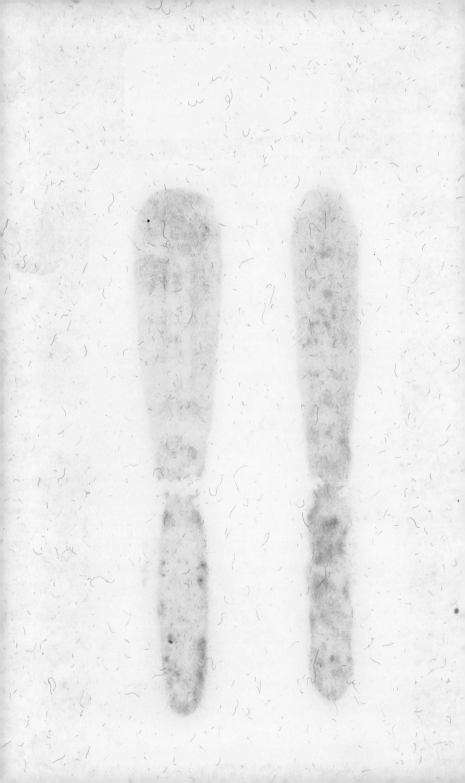

The
I. G.
Beckoning
Dream

The Beckoning Dream

Evelyn Berckman

THORNDIKE PRESS • THORNDIKE, MAINE

Library of Congress Cataloging in Publication Data:

Berckman, Evelyn.
  The beckoning dream.

  Reprint. Originally published: New York : New American Library, 1955.
  1. Large type books. I. Title.
[PS3552.E68B4   1983]   813'.54   83-17862
ISBN 0-89621-483-4

Large Print edition available through arrangement with Dodd Mead and Company.

Cover design by Andy Winther

CHAPTER 1

The dream shocked through Mr. Archibald
Gedney with its customary disagreeable
violence, from his nerve-centres to his outermost fingertips, jerking his arms and legs for a
fraction of a second and bringing him full
awake. He lay sweating heavily and breathing
fast, his eyes darting about wildly like an
elderly frightened bird's — until his surroundings could once more take shape, and by
their familiarity calm him down again. This
process usually took the better part of thirty
seconds, and the present time was no excep-
tion; his heartbeat steadied gradually, his gaze
became more peaceful and wandered here and
there as he lay on his wheelbed, standing on
the perfect lawn of the small, very expensive
nursing-home (Minimum Fee Three Hundred
Dollars per Week, Minimum Stay of Guest
One Month, Admission Through Personal
Physician Only).

It had been a warm day for late October,

and the setting sun, clearcut, fell regularly down a radiant sky without a single cloud. The light flamed, the earth flamed in answer; the grass was of a green so luminous and piercing that he had to close his eyes against it. Then he stole one more glance, quick and furtive, to see whether his sudden waking had attracted the attention of any of the nurses on duty. It had not, he perceived with relief, though they were a most vigilant lot of women, for all their air of calm and relaxation as they sat or strolled here and there as if among the guests at a garden party, instead of among the patients of a fancy sanitarium. But the nearest white figure was quite a distance off, for the grounds were farflung, with almost the reach of a park, and the patients were sparsely dotted about in the perfectly-tended vastness. Privacy, almost the greatest of all luxuries, was well understood in this place; he could shut his eyes in peace and think about THE DREAM.

For thus, in his mind's eye, he saw it — in capital letters — and reflected that if it were not the father and mother of all recurrent dreams, it ought to be. It had begun nearly twelve years ago — after the occurrence that he had trained himself never to think of — and for the last couple of years he had dreamed hardly anything else. It was always the same; always unwinding itself deliberately, neither faster nor slower; first in a long dark coil of cowardice and greed, then of acute apprehension. Finally would come the shock of terror as the cataclysm approached – and at this point he always woke up. For years he had wondered: what was this undisclosed climax? was it discovery? punishment? But actually there had been no discovery and no punishment; they had gotten away with it. He remembered his share in it with shame and revulsion, for his share had been passive, not active. Not for him the dignity, however atrocious, of action, of the deed; only the meanness of skulking on the fringes while it was done, only the queasiness of complicity. And from there his thoughts travelled, logically, to Myra.

Myra. Myra, who had planned it all from the beginning, and then – trust her – had carefully involved the four of them, on the premise that if all were to benefit, all should share the hazard. She had bullied and argued them into line; she had carefully dictated their various rôles in the proceeding. It was sound strategy, her warning them not to confide their instructions to each other; then, if anything went wrong, no one could betray too much from his limited knowledge. It was like Myra to have conceived and carried through that project.

Almost from infancy she had been the only forceful one among the four Gedney children — apart from Theodore, with his fat-boy possessiveness. Luanna, the eldest, then he, Archibald, had been more or less alike; weedy, lackadaisical, not robust. At this remove of time, he saw them all — with merciless clarity — as betrayed into Myra's hands by their native weaknesses, by the rotten spots in their characters; by laziness, cowardice, sickness of waiting, sickness of greed. Yes, Myra had fulfilled her early promise when, at the age of fifty-three, she had instigated and committed that crime which, thereafter, had regularly and monotonously supplied the raw material of THE DREAM.

"Damn her," he thought, for the ten thousandth time in twelve years; his bitter, lacerating hatred had never lessened. Damn Myra, who had poisoned his life; his health had begun to fail immediately after the — the occurrence. For he possessed neither sufficient callousness nor power of forgetfulness to profit by a killing; he had no stomach for money gained in such a manner. The trouble was, he had not realized this in time, and now appeared in his own eyes as a disgusting and cowardly old man who had accepted the fruits of murder, then whined about the consequences.

Well, if suffering were any atonement – which he doubted – he had certainly suffered; serve him right, a thousand times over.

But how did she do it? he thought. *How did she do it?* He had battered himself against that question for twelve years; exhaustingly, futilely. How could Myra, of all people, commit a murder and have it pass the scrutiny of trained eyes, of expert examination? He remembered the doctor's dissatisfaction, his request for the family's consent to an autopsy; he remembered Myra's ready agreement, her peaceful air, her total lack of alarm, though he and the rest of them, he knew, were shaking in their shoes – dissolving into mere cold puddles of terror. Myra in connection with undiscoverable poisons or drugs – the thought was laughable, for Myra was a profoundly ignorant woman. That is, she knew all about clothes, cosmetics, cars, liquor and bridge and luxurious travel accommodation, but he doubted whether she had read a book in her life; and as for her education, it had consisted of a desultory attendance at a series of smart schools, from which she had emerged with an excellent seat on a horse and little else, as far as he could recollect. From what source did such a woman derive the knowledge to commit an undetectable murder? Grotesque; and the more he thought about it, the more he came up against the stone wall of the utterly unsolvable.

An accession of weakness diverted his attention; a peculiar, mortal weakness, an airiness yet leadenness in his joints, so that he felt nailed down to his bed, rather than lying upon it. Obviously he would not live long, and this conviction, in turn, set him wondering whether the secret would die with him. Presumably it would; unlikely that anyone would unearth it, at this late date. Luanna was fading into senility, or so he understood, not having seen her for years; Theo would keep his mouth shut, pop-eyed apprehensive slug that he was, inbedded in the fat of the land. As for Myra — Mr. Gedney laughed to himself, a gasping, lungless laugh. Myra was as immune from remorse as a diamond, with which she shared a comparable degree of hardness. No doubt she had forgotten the whole episode years ago. Myra was safe from the misery that had eaten him hollow, safe from the scourgings of THE DREAM.

His private incubus; this again gave his thoughts a new direction. When a man died, what happened to his dreams? Did they die with him, necessarily? For some dreams have such vividness, such solidity, as to seem possessed of an independent existence somewhere, apart from the dreamer's. His own dream, for instance; so leaden was it, so ponderable, that he felt it should materialize visibly above his head at times, like a balloon from the mouth of a comic-strip character. With all his heart he yearned to bequeath this torture to Myra — to all of them; *I give and devise the torment of* THE DREAM *to my sisters Myra and Luanna and my brother Theodore . . .* he started laughing, silently, at himself. Here he was, a voiceless Rigoletto without accompaniment, hurling an ineffectual curse . . . he was no more than two centuries behind the times, at any rate.

All of a sudden, something very strange was happening within Mr. Gedney; strange but also intensely familiar, an immemorial acquaintance, implicit in life's beginning no less than its end. Extinction began flooding up into his head and outward to his extremities — but there was no fear, he noted, with the mind's strange detachment, no fear at all. It was very well arranged; you were so astounded, so engrossed with the finality working within you, that you forgot to be afraid. Then a sort of pins-and-needles began all over his body, as when one's foot went to sleep — the blood stopping, of course, but it tickled so excruciatingly that he felt himself smiling. With the fading edge of his consciousness he knew that here was the explanation of that famed convention, the dying smile: no vision of seraphs, or of dear faces gone before — you were merely being tickled, literally, to death. Dimly he reflected that this piece of information should be communicated to someone, but in the next moment the power of communicating anything had passed from him.

The sun had almost set, and instantly the autumnal chill began creeping out of the earth; in a leisurely procession of wheelchairs and wheel-beds the patients were being assisted inside. Some were ambulatory, and strolled up to the big, cheerful white mansion, a nurse bringing up the rear.

Miss Trask now approached the bed on which lay Mr. Gedney. What she saw made her check instantly but inconspicuously; the other patients must not be alarmed or depressed. Calmly she put a hand on his wrist, while seeming to speak to him. Then, as calmly, she made an imperceptible signal — standard for such occasions — to Miss Selden, the head nurse, who stood bandying cheerful small-talk with the patients as they drifted past her.

When everyone was inside — and not until

14

then — Miss Selden joined Miss Trask, who was making a feint of wheeling the bed along slowly; she and her patient looking, in the vast expanse of lawn, most peculiarly solitary. With composure she eyed Mr. Gedney, already about two-thirds of his natural size in the mysterious transmutations of death.

"We'll have Dr. Breen look at him," she said, "but there isn't much doubt."

"None at all, I should think," said Miss Trask.

"Well, let's take him in," said Miss Selden, and Miss Trask began pushing the bed with as much unconcern — for the benefit of any chance looker-out-of-windows — as if she were convoying live Mr. Gedney, instead of dead Mr. Gedney.

"I don't know what he was breathing with, toward the last," said Miss Selden thoughtfully.

They exchanged no other word until they arrived, not at the big door leading to the over-size elevator with its whispering imperceptible motion, its warm lights and velvet bench around three sides, but at an inconspicuous side door. This opened upon a bleak passage with a cold smell of cement and antiseptics. Dr. Breen, being summoned, arrived like a shot, but in less than a minute allowed them to consign Mr. Gedney to an attendant, and to make their thankful escape.

Upstairs waited Mr. Gedney's spacious room, warm and comfortable, with its inviting bed, his small leather easy-chairs, his bridge-table – this unused for a long time – his favorite books, his magnifying glass, his diary and desk-set in sumptuous green-and-gold leather. Through a half-open door glimmered the bathroom, in parchment-colored tiles and bright silvery fixtures. But now Mr. Gedney had done with all these amenities, for good.

Miss Selden put down the phone at last, exasperated.

"Well! Some relations our Mr. Gedney had!" she exclaimed to Miss Trask, who had just entered the office.

"On his regular notify-in-case list," said Miss Selden, "he has three names. Miss Luanna, sister, Mr. Theodore Gedney, brother, Mrs. Myra Walworth, sister. Well, I phoned Miss Luanna; it seems she's a chronic invalid and never goes out. I phoned Mr. Theodore; he's in Europe. I called Mrs. Myra, and –" she paused.

"And –?" prodded Miss Trask avidly.

"It seems," said Miss Selden, heavily ironic, "that Mrs. Myra isn't so well either. Well, I must say she sounded perfectly healthy to me."

"You mean she's not coming?" demanded Miss Trask, shocked.

"Not she," returned Miss Selden. "Terribly upset and so forth," she cheeped on a high note, in presumable imitation of Mrs. Myra. "Upset my foot, if she'd have been any calmer she'd be dead. But she's sending her daughter-in-law."

"Didn't someone like that," demanded Miss Trask slowly, with an air of evoking a faint, far-off memory, "use to come visit him, three or four years ago?"

"I wasn't here three or four years ago," Miss Selden pointed out.

"And I wasn't his nurse then — Mona Bradley was, and she left here ages ago," said Miss Trask. "But I *think* I remember Mona saying that none of his family ever came to see him, except just this one woman. Mona said there was something funny about her — something unpleasant — if I remember rightly. I wonder if this woman that's coming is the same one."

"Search me — all that was before my time," said Miss Selden. "Well, I've notified his lawyers, and I suppose she'll be here tomorrow too — the daughter-in-law."

17

CHAPTER 2

Miss Selden was habituated — but not really hardened — to the emotional aftermaths of death, so it was a relief that everything following on Mr. Gedney's demise was in the highest degree impersonal. On the next afternoon a pleasant middle-aged man arrived from the firm of Foulke, Combs and Sturgis, Mr. Gedney's lawyers, and almost on his heels appeared — as announced — Mrs. Connie Walworth. Miss Selden conducted each of them in turn to Mr. Gedney's room, murmured, "Mr. Sinclair, this is Mrs. Walworth, on behalf of Mrs. Myra Walworth," and tactfully left them together.

"Good-day," said Connie, in a clear, peculiarly timbreless voice. "I'm Mrs. Walworth's daughter-in-law."

"Ah yes," said Mr. Sinclair, who obviously had not been able to place her. He bowed, then stood for a moment undecided.

"Just go on with what you were doing," said

Connie. "Don't let me interrupt you."

She sat down in one of the handsome red leather chairs (cataloguing it mentally, on the instant, as certainly no property of the sanitarium's) then unslung from her shoulder the strap of her enormous green alligator bag, set it on the floor beside the chair, and took out a cigarette and a beautiful gold lighter.

"Just go ahead," she repeated, as he still seemed to hesitate. "Don't mind me."

"Well —" Mr. Sinclair's deprecating gesture took in the whole room "— I'll have to go through all this rather thoroughly, you understand —?"

"Naturally," Connie acquiesced. "That's what you're here for." She lit the cigarette and sat seemingly inattentive; in reality she was closely following his every action: First he investigated the desk; then the dresser, with an embarrassed smile sliding his hand beneath and between the immaculate rows of handkerchiefs, shirts, underlinen.

"People sometimes secrete valuables in places like this," he explained. "Have to make sure."

"Of course," she said. Then, as he opened the door of the enormous closet, she rose, strolled over, and stood looking on.

"Archie did himself well, for an old maid,"

she thought, eyeing the rows of corduroy, flannel and tweed jackets — superlative tailoring and fabrics if she knew anything about it, and she knew a good deal. In the background, his dinner clothes appeared dimly through a plastic container; on the door itself hung his cap, his cane, his light topcoat of cream-colored camel's-hair. She gathered a fold of this in her hand and crushed it; it felt like face-powder. She released it, and the fabric sprang back again, without a single mark.

"Three hundred and fifty at least," she thought to herself.

Mr. Sinclair emerged at last from the closet, having conscientiously explored everything. It had not taken long, in such meticulous order was the closet kept.

"Nothing there," he announced, seemed to reflect a moment, then picked up the phone. When someone answered, he said, "Did Mr. Gedney store any luggage here, trunks or —? Oh? Well, could you have them brought to his room right away? and don't forget anything, please? Thank you." He started to hang up, then added hastily, "And tell me, did he keep anything in the sanitarium safe? papers —? nothing at all? thank you." He hung up this time, and a waiting interval followed which Connie, smoking, made no effort to enliven.

Mr. Sinclair moved about aimlessly and at last ventured, "Very sad, these occasions."

"Why sad?" returned Connie, with unemphasized contempt. "He was way in his seventies, wasn't he? That's a good long time to live — for anyone."

"Ah yes, but the — the things people leave," bumbled Mr. Sinclair, motioning about him. "The things they used — poignant somehow, I always think."

"Patek Philippe," murmured Connie as if in answer, reading from the face of a watch lying on the dresser — a miraculous thing, a mere sliver of platinum. She flicked him a covertly sardonic glance, and he said hastily, "How's Mrs. Walworth, these days?"

"All right as far as I know," said Connie. "She only rings me up if she needs me, or wants me to do anything. Otherwise, I don't see much of her." She added, at Mr. Sinclair's slight look of perplexity, "I used to see her oftener — of course — when my husband was alive."

"Ah," said Mr. Sinclair, with a look of enlightenment, "I didn't know Mrs. Walworth had lost a son."

"Why should you?" returned Connie, entirely composed. "Unless you knew her well."

"I don't," he mumbled. "I've seen her at various times, but I don't know her."

At this point, to his obvious relief, came the knock; he called "Come in!" and an attendant, entering in silence, made a rapid pile of three suitcases and a wardrobe trunk which he unloaded from a dolly, then went out again, shutting the door. The luggage, parchment cowhide with heavy locks and silver name-plates, was gaily patched with foreign labels, from which shone brightly here and there the white-and-scarlet 1ST CLASS stickers of the Cunard line. Mr. Sinclair opened them, one after another; they were unlocked and entirely empty.

"Well —" he straightened "— that's the lot, I guess — that does it."

Connie watched him as he stood staring before him and rattling the change in his pocket. In her mind she was forming and reforming a question, the single question that had possessed her utterly from the moment she had heard of Archie's death; the question that she had no right to ask, not being one of the immediate family. Nevertheless she opened her mouth to speak, then closed it as Mr. Sinclair moved toward the dresser, touched the watch lying there, then opened a glossy leather box sitting beside it. This, being opened, proved to contain a half-dozen pairs of cuff-links in chaste designs, some gold and some platinum, and, in a little compartment of their own, five obviously real pearls, his dress studs and links. There was also a gold-and-platinum money-clasp, and nothing else.

"These things," he observed pessimistically, "won't bring a third of what he paid for them." He moved to the desk, opened a drawer; it contained neat stacks of diaries in the same binding as the one lying on the desk. A gold-stamped date – *1944* – caught Connie's eye.

"Believe it or not," said Mr. Sinclair, "I've riffled through all of these. People often hide money or documents in books – though it would be out of character for Mr. Gedney. But I had to make sure." Absently, from the desk-top, he picked up the current diary – with its slender gold date – and leafed its pages rapidly.

"Take this to Mrs. Walworth, why don't you?" he urged, the notion seeming to strike him suddenly. "The valuable stuff'll have to wait for the appraiser, but some little memento like this – she might like to have her brother's diary, eh? for sentimental reasons?"

"Thank you," said Connie gravely, taking the diary and holding back a wolfish grin at the notion of Myra's wanting anything for sentimental reasons. She picked up her bag, then ventured on a preliminary inquiry, by way of leading up to the major issue. "How long –" she was widening the mouth of the bag on its leather drawstrings "– how long do you think it'll take to settle the estate?"

"Estate?" Mr. Sinclair echoed. "My dear lady, exclusive of the effects in this room, Mr. Gedney's estate only amounts to –" at this point he remembered Connie's standing as a relative by law only; his mouth clamped shut, his features became professionally inscrutable. "There shouldn't be too much delay in settling the estate," he observed smoothly. "Not more than usual, at any rate."

She hardly heard him, so intent was she on her next inquiry. By no means unaware of his self-interruption and his sudden reserve, she could not be deflected from the life-and-death matter, the essential question; she would scream if she waited any longer, purgatoried on this knife-edge anxiety. It was going to sound awkward, not casual, as she had wished – but no matter.

"What'll they do next?" she demanded, her chest painfully tight. "Read the will, or what?"

"Will?" Mr. Sinclair echoed again. "There is no will. Mr. Gedney died intestate."

She stood looking at him, her whole body

dissolving; the blackness of shock swam up before her eyes. The diary, unnoticed, fell from her suddenly nerveless hand into the bag.

"Are you sure?" she said lightly.

"Pretty sure," said Mr. Sinclair. "It's not in this room, and he lived here for the past five years. He didn't maintain residence elsewhere. He had nothing in storage, he had no lockbox, his bankbooks and statements and checkbooks are in that drawer —" he indicated the desk "— and that's all there is, apparently."

Connie was silent, consumed by a wild longing to pick up the phone standing between them and dash it into his face — upon his rimless glasses for choice.

"Actually," the old fool was saying, "what I'm here for mostly is to look for a will." He said something else, his voice reaching her as from a great distance . . . she would vomit in a moment, she would topple in a faint . . . casually she moved to a chair and sat down.

"I'm a little surprised," she began, taking out a cigarette with steady hands and looking up at him amiably. "You see, my husband was his only nephew, and they were pretty thick, and Archie promised Bruce — definitely — that whatever he had would come to him. Then when Bruce died, Archie promised he'd do *something* for me, at least. I didn't ask him — he mentioned it more than once, of his own accord. I'd visit him here, and he'd talk about it." She paused, feeling like death, and smiled brightly at Mr. Sinclair. "So seeing that he promised me, only four years ago . . ."

"Four years ago," mused Mr. Sinclair. "You hadn't seen him more recently than that?"

"No — because he himself practically asked me to stop coming," Connie explained. This was about half-true; the request had not been made in very great earnest, and she failed to mention with what relief and alacrity she had acceded to it. "Well, after that, I could only do as he said."

Mr. Sinclair nodded, noncommittal.

"So I'm wondering," she went on, "if there isn't a will somewhere, and it just hasn't turned up yet."

"I'm afraid not," said Mr. Sinclair. "Our Mr. Combs was always after him to make one. If it existed, we'd have drawn it up for him. If he'd left a holograph will, it would be in this room, and you can rest assured that it isn't. No, Mrs. Walworth, if he promised you and then didn't make a will after all, it's too bad, but . . ." his voice trailed off; tactfully he omitted to point out that her degree of relationship gave her no claim at all, for he realized there was no need. Both were silent for some moments, while

Connie in her mind damned Archie to obscene and unimaginable hells.

"He did himself well, while he had his health," meditated Mr. Sinclair, his eyes going from the clothes-closet to the superb luggage. "And when he didn't have it —" he glanced about the spacious room "— he still made himself fairly cozy. Well, why not? He could afford to."

"He certainly could," said Connie, with a bite in her voice like sulphuric acid. "There were four of them, and they got a quarter-million apiece — my husband told me."

"Not quite a quarter-million," corrected Mr. Sinclair. "It might have been that, if old Mrs. Gedney hadn't lived so long. 'Way up in the eighties, wasn't she? They couldn't inherit until she died, and she must have used up a good bit of the estate. Well, well, so Mr. Archie didn't beat his mother's time, in the end."

"She wasn't his mother," Connie said absently, her thoughts elsewhere. "She wasn't the mother of any of them."

"Their step-mother, I mean," concurred Mr. Sinclair. "Their father married twice — I'd forgotten." He slowly put on his topcoat, picked up his hat. "Are you coming now, Mrs. Walworth, or —?"

"I'm coming," said Connie, and rose. At this moment came a tap at the door, and being bidden, Miss Selden looked in. Another nurse was visible behind her.

"I thought, if you were through," she said, professionally dulcet, "— if we could talk to Mrs. Walworth for a minute —"

"We're through," said Mr. Sinclair. "I've the inventory, and the appraiser'll come tomorrow. Well, goodday, Mrs. Walworth — ladies."

He walked downstairs rather than ring for the elevator, thinking of Connie Walworth. There was no doubt in his mind that the news about the will — or the absence of one — had been a mortal blow to her. Still, she had taken it well; she had nerve. Also, surprisingly, he realized all the implications of her tweed suit, her brogues, her gloves, her superb bag; all these, once the very best of their kind, were scuffed and subtly out of shape, in urgent need of replacement. Mr. Sinclair's marriage had been one long grapple with an extravagant wife, and he knew more about female trappings than might be supposed, by the look of him. But from long habit he never confided his impressions to others; his thoughts were his own.

"I thought," said Miss Selden, "you might

like to know something about Mr. Gedney's passing — so you could tell Mrs. Walworth, you know."

"Certainly," said Connie, with a burlesque solemnity so overdone that it seemed as if the two women must get it. No fear of that, though; not those two old bags.

"There was no pain," said Miss Selden. "This is Miss Trask, Mr. Gedney's regular nurse, and she'll tell you he passed quite peacefully, didn't he, Blanche?"

"Yes — he just went to sleep," confirmed Miss Trask.

"That's good," murmured Connie, wanting to scream with laughter.

"I thought it might be a comfort to Mrs. Walworth if she knew," said Miss Selden. "Was there anything else his family ought to know, Blanche?"

"Well, everyone liked him," said Miss Trask, and Miss Selden chimed in, "Yes, everyone did. The loveliest manners, and so *considerate!*"

"There were those dreams, of course," the Trask maundered on. "Nightmares all the time. They wore him out a good deal, but still, you can't compare that to physical suffering, can you?"

Connie agreed that you could not, and rose. In another moment some savagery would get past her lips, and dearly as she would love to see their stupefaction, she did not quite dare. They came with her to the elevator, where she managed to shake them off and go down alone.

The instant the whispering cage fell from sight, Miss Trask exclaimed, "That's the woman — the same woman Mona told me about. I'd swear to it — I'm sure. Something poisonous about her, she always said, and such horrible eyes — it's got to be the same one. Did you notice her eyes?"

"I couldn't miss them," said Miss Selden, "but beside all that, there's something else about her — something I just can't put my finger on —"

"Mona used to say that," declared Miss Trask. "I felt it too — from the first."

But, after comparing notes for some moments, they were unable to define the precise nature of Mrs. Walworth's disturbing quality.

CHAPTER 3

Connie Walworth suffered from no lack of intelligence; her mind — when she chose to use it — was as sharp as a razor, and as inhuman. Her other traits were a pathological laziness, love of luxury, and a fixed conviction that the cream of existence was hers by right. In addition, all her faculties were bent inward upon herself in a concentration rapt and unbroken, and she had a fund of hatred, ever-ready and sincere, for anyone who diverted her to any extent from this self-communion.

However, the events of the last hour had violently ruptured her almost impenetrable complacency. The news of Archie's death, on the previous day, had appeared in the light of fantastic luck, of providential, last-minute rescue from her frightfully precarious situation. She had counted on inheritance, and she had a right to count on it, she told herself furiously. He had promised her, he had *promised* her, the old — (here she applied a surprising word to the dead man): he had let her down utterly. Her mind skimmed lightly over the fact that the promise had been extremely indefinite, made at a moment of great physical weakness and distress, after his nephew's death; she closed her eyes likewise to the possibility that she had merely misconstrued some word of Archie's into a promise. Over the years the episode had built itself up in her mind, more and more firmly, into definite expectations, a settled affair; he had lied to her, betrayed her, the horrid old man, wallowing in luxury up to his neck, smothered in comfort, with his cashmere coats and platinum watches and whatnot, and never even giving her a thought, damn his soul. She wished he had had a hard death instead of an easy one; no torment could be more than he deserved. She spared, in passing, a fulminating epithet for that close-mouthed lawyer back there in the room, with his refusal — no less insulting for being unspoken — to reveal the least fact as to the amount of Archie's estate; she was one of the sacred Gedneys only by marriage, not entitled to know anything. Out of the welter of her thoughts, one stony fact confronted her, inescapable; she would get nothing out of this death. She had been banking on it for a long time, and she would get absolutely nothing.

She shifted the strap of the alligator bag, in which reposed, beside a mass of impedimenta, exactly three dollars and thirty-eight cents — literally every penny she had in the world. With her graceful light step she reached the parking-space where stood her Lincoln convertible, bought second-hand a long time ago — a flashy special-color job in cream, with poison-green leather upholstery; urgently and immediately needing, as she knew only too well, about three hundred dollars' worth of work on the engine. Before the gleaming thing stood two neat, well-mannered blonde children, son and daughter of the very serious and religious Scotch gardener, who lived on the grounds. The boy had just reached out and with a careful forefinger was stroking the satiny enamel when Connie appeared.

"All right, you little bastards," she said. "Beat it." She got in as the children stood uncomprehending but aghast; the heavy door slammed and the car roared to life and down the drive. She was doing sixty before the next turn, and screamed around it on two wheels, then came blasting down the narrow road — a secondary road — at seventy. She longed to smash something, destroy something under the wheels; chickens and a dog had a narrow escape. Then a small chipmunk darted out in front of her, turned once, terrified, turned again, was lost. The car jolted minutely and rushed on, leaving a bas-relief chipmunk flattened into the road, a gay red ribbon of gut flung out from its underside.

The episode gave her a savage satisfaction, calmed her somewhat. At a more decorous rate of speed, about a half-hour later, she pulled into the driveway of an enormous old-fashioned house with turrets and a porte-cochère. Here successive generations of Gedneys had lived since 1890, and here still resided Miss Luanna Gedney, an unmarried lady of seventy-eight, eldest of the four Gedney inheritors. Connie rang a bell, waited impatiently, rang again. Hurried footsteps were faintly audible within; the door was plucked open.

"Oh, goodday, Mrs. Connie." Mrs. Donlan's strong Irish accent emerged between puffs and pants. "I'm sorry to keep you waiting –" she stood aside as Connie came in "– but I was upstairs with her, an' it's such distances in this big old barn of a place. Were you wantin' to see her?"

"I'd better," said Connie. "Her brother Archibald died yesterday – at the sanitarium – and my mother-in-law thought she'd better be told." *Save it, you old fool,* she thought, at

Mrs. Donlan's cluck of commiseration. "Do you think there's any chance she'll understand?"

"Well now, I don't know," said Mrs. Donlan consideringly. "She had a bad night last night, a very bad night — callin' out all the time with these turrible dreams. Now that's somethin' entirely new with her, dreamin' like that; I never knew it happen before. 'No, I won't, Myra!' she kept hollerin'. 'No, no, we mustn't!' — An' she's not over it yet, she's still upset — so it's annybody's guess will she understand you or not, Mrs. Connie, annybody's guess."

"Still, I'd better try," said Connie, and rapidly ascended the baronial oak staircase with its shallow treads, its landing with the huge stained-glass window and group of entwined nymphs in marble, and more shallow steps. Then she went down a wide carpeted hall, Mrs. Donlan laboring in her wake, and opened the glossy cream-painted door upon the master bedroom. This was vast, with two deep bays, a fireplace, and an acre of gleaming floor almost covered with Oriental scatter-rugs. Luanna's bed was not even conspicuous in its lordly dimensions, and Mrs. Donlan's bed, in a far angle of the room, was hardly noticeable. In the fireplace a big fire purred and occasionally snapped; the room was airy and pleasant.

"She does love the fire," commented Mrs. Donlan. "So I have one for her most times, seein' it's little pleasure she gets."

Connie approached the bed; here lay Miss Luanna Gedney, silver-haired and well-fleshed, her complexion clear and healthily pale, for there was nothing at all wrong with Miss Luanna but second childhood. She lay staring up at Connie as she approached, but made no sound nor movement.

"She don't quite know you yet, but she will, maybe," said Mrs. Donlan, then cooed, "Miss Lu, here's a visitor for you, lamb. Here's Mrs. Connie, duckie, you know Mrs. Connie?"

The unwinking stare was still nailed upon Connie, but into it now came a look of horror.

"Myra . . ." articulated the figure on the bed.

"Ah, she's takin' you for her sister Myra," explained Mrs. Donlan unnecessarily; then to Luanna, "Not Mrs. Myra, lamb, it's Mrs. Connie! — She's still got that dream in her mind, looks like," she muttered in a rapid aside, "but try tellin' her now, go on an' try."

"Aunt Luanna," said Connie quickly and loudly, feeling the same sick distaste as on her rare visits to the sanitarium. "Uncle Archie died yesterday. Uncle Archibald — dead."

"Yer brother Archibald," Mrs. Donlan amplified. "He died yesterday —" she stopped in consternation as tears began sliding down the old lady's face. "Ah, he's happy, Miss Lu, he's galm to Heaven —"

"Dead!" Luanna's sudden outcry shrilled across Mrs. Donlan's utterance, striking her silent with astonishment. "She's dead?" Her voice, slurred and stumbling, struggled forth with a desperate urgency. "What'll they do to us, Myra? what'll they do to us?"

"Now what's this?" demanded Mrs. Donlan, nonplussed, and bent down soothingly. But Luanna's stare remained riveted on Connie in an anguish of fear, and the river of half-distorted words kept tumbling out of her mouth. "I didn't want to!" she blubbered. "It's you . . . made me steal it, Myra. Sharp, sharp!" She shivered with a violent revulsion. "The . . . the needle . . . I hate . . . I hate it. . . ."

"There's no needle!" Mrs. Donlan expostulated. "She's deathly afraid of the needle," she said in a low voice to Connie. "She makes the rare old fuss, the times the doctor has to give her one, like she was frightened of her life —"

"You — you made me!" Luanna's wail interrupted. "And now she's . . . she's dead!"

Then exhaustion suddenly, visibly overcame her; she seemed to collapse where she lay. "Dead, dead," she mumbled. "What'll we do? she's dead."

"Not she — *he*," said Connie. "Archibald, Aunt Luanna, Archibald died —"

"Mrs. Connie." Mrs. Donlan quickly touched her arm. "Let it go — she can't understand, an' it's only bad for her." She beckoned; they moved toward the corner of the vast room, out of sight of the bed. "I never knew her take on like this," she muttered rapidly. "It's that nightmare she had last night. Maybe she's gettin' violent, I don't know. Could you make it out, what she was sayin'?"

Connie, bored, shook her head.

"She thinks she *stole* somethin'!" the other went on. "That's plain nonsensical. But these old wans that's got a screw loose, they take a notion into their heads an' you can't —" she checked as the door opened slowly and a short stout woman entered, carrying a tray.

"Here's her little supper," said Mrs. Donlan, "Let's us go downstairs the while Aggie's with her. — Here's yer supper, lamb," she called cheerfully, toward the bed. "Here's yer nice supper."

She held the door open for Connie and followed her downstairs, silent until they reached the big entrance-hall.

"Well, I guess she didn't understand about Mr. Archibald," she said. "Maybe it's just as well."

"I daresay," said Connie absently, her glance ranging about her.

"— but this wakin' me up four an' five times a night —" Mrs. Donlan was saying. "If my rest's broken like that, we'll have to have a night-nurse. I've got to have my rest, Mrs. Connie, I'm tied to her pretty close, daytimes. There's plenty of money for a nurse or anything else that's needful, praise be," she ended with a jolly laugh odious in the ears of Connie, who was regarding the series of enormous rooms opening on the hall. They all looked dead, unlived-in, but were scrupulously dusted and clean.

"It's mad, her living in this place all by herself," she could not forbear observing. "Mrs. Walworth says it was too big when the four of them were children here."

Mrs. Donlan bridled faintly. *What business is it of yours?* she demanded mentally. Aloud she said, "This is her home, Mrs. Connie, she'll live here an' die here — she's used to it, she couldn't stand no change. You needn't worry about her," she said smoothly, with deliberate malice. "It's the grand care she gets, between me an' Aggie. The doctor says she's in wonderful shape, she might outlive all of us."

She let Connie out and followed her progress down the walk with hard eyes. This job was a stronghold, a corporate possession of herself and Aggie, her sister; they would defend it to the last ditch. A job where there was absolutely no supervision, no one giving orders, and very high pay — gladly given by the bank that was Miss Luanna's guardian — for they were increasingly indispensable to the senile old lady. They lived high at no expense, with every comfort and luxury, including — on Sundays, and by spelling each other — that of the ten-thirty Mass instead of the seven-thirty. All this hinged on one thing — the continued existence of Miss Luanna Gedney. And if Miss Luanna could reach the age of a hundred by means of their combined efforts, such combined effort would assuredly not be lacking.

Connie got into the car and sat there, looking at the enormous house and wide, well-kept grounds. All that, she thought incredulously, all that maintained, kept up — to house one feeble-minded old bag of bones. Two people taking care of her, and now possibly a third — to say nothing of the outside help. To think what all that meant, in terms of money! Fresh from her experience at the sanitarium, Connie was extraordinarily sensitive to this aspect of it. Rivers of money, she thought wildly, as the car started moving; money being poured out for half-witted Luanna while she herself, literally, was desperate for a few dollars. All her former rage returned, her raw resentment companioned by disappointment and despair, and in these narrow and closely-settled suburban streets she could have no recourse to her usual method of blowing off steam — driving at crazy speed. In this mood, and in a dangerously pent-up state of explosiveness — needing only a touch to set it off — she rolled up a driveway and stopped on the turnaround behind a pleasant small house, some stone but mostly white shingle, with a sleek green lawn framed by a barberry hedge, brilliantly red. Here lived Connie's mother-in-law, Mrs. Myra Walworth.

CHAPTER 4

The front door was slightly ajar on this mild day, and the screen door unlatched; Connie stepped into the little hall, darkish, where a man she had never seen before was putting on his topcoat. Her expert eye registered all his good points in an instant; medium-tall (she did not like very tall men), good build, broad shoulders; dark eyes, dark vigorous hair, face not handsome but full of masculinity; everything about him was hard and masculine, and he was not over thirty-two or three.

"Another of Myra's — my God, how does she do it?" she thought sardonically, until he picked up a doctor's satchel which the hall-table had blocked from her view.

"Good day," she said agreeably.

"Good day," he responded, then took up his hat and grinned slightly. "Well — goodbye."

"Doctor —?" she said quickly. Her impulse to detain him was pure instinct, several jumps ahead of calculation.

"Dr. Markham."

"I'm Connie Walworth, Mrs. Walworth's daughter-in-law," she offered. "Who's sick here?"

"Mrs. Walworth had a couple of heart spasms recently." His voice was hard, compelling, with a slightly ironic undercurrent; she felt a pleasant little shiver as she asked. "Anything serious?"

"Well, she's sixty-five," said the doctor. "Anything wrong when you're over sixty has to be reckoned with. But it's a very minor condition — not the sort of thing that knocks you over one day for keeps — nothing like that." He paused a moment, thinking; she waited, looking at him, feeling that slight agreeable sickness that was always — with her — the precursor of being strongly attracted.

"There's some pain attached to these occasional attacks of hers, but we can control that pretty well," the doctor was going on. "You needn't worry — her cardiogram shows up pretty well for her age, and she's being very cooperative about this. She'll live a long time yet."

"That's good," murmured Connie, hardly hearing a word he said. She had not felt what she called *the wildness* for a man, a long time now; after the disaster of a few hours ago, she

43

was more than in the mood for wildness of some kind. She watched his lips, unconscious of the words they formed, waking in time to listen as he concluded, "– the only danger for her now is agitation of any kind – emotional upsets – anger or worry, fear, anxiety, anything like that."

"Myra's never upset," she smiled, holding his eyes with her own. He was looking at her now with a different look, he was conscious of her; her heart began a fierce victorious racing. It was going to happen as she wanted, sooner rather than later, and she had not been so drawn to a man for a couple of years. Lazily she half-drooped her lids, then opened her eyes very wide – a manoeuvre she had always found dependable – as she went on, "She could give lessons to a cucumber – that's the kind Myra is. Good day, doctor."

She ascended the stairs quickly and gracefully; without turning her head, she felt his eyes on her all the way up.

She was much too slender for her height, Ralph Markham reflected, but she was so small-boned that this was hardly apparent. Flat delicate waist, little flesh on her ribs – which made her breasts look all the larger. Thin and voluptuous, a type he had liked more in his experimental youth than he did now. This one moved like a young girl, but there was no doubt to his professional eye, that she was thirty or over. Her nose was a bit too whittled, but her thin lips were somehow disturbing, and her eyes – her eyes were her best point; long, a trifle slanted at the ends, luminous in the dim hall. Light blue or light grey, he supposed; outlined with dark thick lashes, overarched with dark thin brows. But the encounter had left him with a general impression that he did not really like her. This decision he shrugged aside in the same moment that he made it. Whether he liked her or not, there she was, available if he wanted her, and the discontents of his present existence prompted him to accept any diversions that offered, even those not especially congenial. He half-smiled, fairly certain that this hot number would make it her business to be present on the occasion of his next visit to Mrs. Walworth; if not, twenty to one she would get in touch with him some other way. All right, that suited him. Let her do all the chasing, he need not lift a finger; it was being handed to him on a silver platter. He had been working hard without a let-up, an unrelieved gloom pervaded his personal life at the moment, and he could do with a little hell-raising. No need to wait for it very long, either; that suited him, too.

The slight smile was still on his face as he got into his car. He was just about to press the starter — when a curious hiatus took him, a moment of suspension; he sat motionless, aware of an odd unease, as though something unpleasant had just brushed against him. The sensation seemed to connect, in some manner, with Connie Walworth. . . . But the impression, formless and evanescent, was more than dissipated in the next few moments by a profane interlude with the starter. First it would respond to his foot with an agreeable rhythmic vibration, then it would stall; this happened two or three times before he could get moving, and the car was all but new. He had had this trouble with it almost from the first, and was permanently too short of time to have it corrected.

CHAPTER 5

Connie reached the second floor, over the whole of which Myra had spread herself — a feat not so difficult as it sounded, for it comprised the occupation of only three rooms and two baths. One room was her bedroom, another her dressing-room, another her small sitting-room — which accounted for the somewhat odd arrangement by which her daughter, Ann, occupied a first-floor room originally designed as a library or den. For a bathroom Ann used the minute lavatory squeezed in next to the coatroom, and once, daily, went upstairs for her tub, and had never been heard to complain about this disposition of matters.

Myra, for all her attractions, had chalked up only two marriages, the first far back in the mists of time and nearly forgotten by everyone, the second with Tony Walworth, big, handsome, and a heavy drinker. Two children, Bruce and Ann, were the result of this matrimonial essay, indeed its only evidence, for

Tony himself had ended his career by taking that bad curve outside Hargesville at eighty, years and years ago. Apparently Myra had made no really constructive attempt toward a third marriage – though Connie had heard family rumors of a red-hot affair, during the War period, with what she called "some sort of Spick" – who had been, actually, a handsome and dashing Argentinian, with the *réclame* of diplomatic missions in Italy and Germany behind him. But the Argentinian seemed to have faded from the picture. In any case, all this had happened long before Connie's advent into the Gedney and Walworth families by way of her marriage to Bruce. Since the day of that marriage Myra had entertained for Connie a steady, smiling hatred which could hardly have been more virulent if Connie had kidnapped and murdered her only son, instead of merely marrying him. Connie was accurately aware of her mother-in-law's sentiments toward her, and reciprocated them in kind, though the outward communication between them appeared reasonably affable.

"Myra?" called Connie, at the top of the stairs.

"In here!" Myra fluted, and Connie entered the bedroom, a kaleidoscope of pastel taffetas and light – brilliant splintered light off silver, crystal and mirrors; suave bloom of light filtering in softly through fragile apricot drapes. In the midst of this, repairing her face at the dressing-table, sat Myra Walworth.

Myra was a miracle, of the kind produced daily by care and money. She was small (*petite* was her word for it) with a rather square little face, very fair skin marvelously made up and appearing quite unlined, blue eyes, a tip-tilted nose, and singularly pretty lips, whose fullness and shape suggested a mouth permanently pursed for a kiss. All this was framed by a mop of short red ringlets, which Connie never beheld without a silent tribute to Myra's hair-dresser. It was almost impossible to avoid an artificial look with dyed red hair, to say nothing of the hard, old, ghastly look it gave its possessor; but Myra's Felix always turned the trick somehow, and Myra's curls looked almost natural, soft and young – but in some deft way not too young. Then her figure was still quite pretty, with the mere beginnings of telltale slackness in the lines of the bust; the all-over effect was that of an attractive woman in her mid-forties, which was not too bad for one over sixty-five.

"Sit down, pet," she caroled gaily, at sight of her daughter-in-law. "Was it grim? Tell me all

— or rather," she amended, "you'd like a drink first?"

"I wouldn't mind," said Connie, in sardonic understatement, and stepped from the bedroom across the hall, and into Myra's sitting-room. Here she extracted some ice from a microscopic refrigerator in the lower part of an Americanized credenza, and from its upper compartment took at random a bottle of rye — Myra never had any but good liquor. From this she poured an extra-stiff drink, and went back to the bedroom with the cold amber cylinder in her hand.

"Sit down," Myra repeated and Connie sat. "Now tell me," she commanded, and listened in silence for the next half-minute.

"Well, you're just repeating what his lawyers have told me already," she commented, at the end of Connie's recital. "They called me this morning — about there being no will, and so forth. It means I'll have to petition for letters of administrations." She preened importantly. "Theo's cabling his permission — they phoned him in Paris — and Luanna's bank is signing for her. So I'll have my hands full for the next few weeks. Why does it always happen to me?"

Connie grinned an inward sardonic grin at this complaint. She knew how dearly Myra loved any bustle or activity, above all that having to do with money; more than ever she was racked with desire to know how much Archibald had left — though the knowledge would do her little good — and again she began framing inquiries that might sound sufficiently casual. Myra's next utterance, however, forestalled her.

"Do you know," she was saying, "that his whole estate only amounts to eighteen or twenty thousand? He went through his two hundred thousand like a hot knife through butter. Would you think it to look at him, that quiet little old Archie? Slyboots. After all the expenses are paid —" she added carelessly, "— I suppose we'll split up fifteen thousand among the three of us — Luanna, Theo and I." She eyed Connie with covert malice, being only too well aware of her daughter-in-law's financial condition. "It's not much —" she was rubbing it in deliberately, Connie knew "— five thousand apiece."

"And of course," Connie could not forbear commenting, poisonously, "— of course you all need it so badly." Then she cursed herself for a fool; letting Myra see she had gotten a rise out of her, as it was plain she had set out to do! Also, at this point, she abandoned her earlier intention of mentioning Archie's promised bequest; why give Myra a chance to laugh in her face?

"Money's always useful," Mrya smiled, obviously enjoying herself to the utmost; then inquired, "And you don't think Luanna understood about Archie?"

"Not a word," said Connie. "All she did was talk nonsense." She changed the subject, "What's this about your having to have a doctor?"

"My sweetie? my Dr. Markham?" Myra responded with rapture. "Did you meet him downstairs? Hands off, honey, he's mine." Her warning was only half-jocular, "Yes, I had a couple of these heart-attacks, sort of, and they scared me, honestly — but here's what he gave me." She opened her bag, took out a squat green bottle full of fluid, and unscrewed its top, from which extended a glass rod about an inch long. "I just take a drop of this when I feel bad," she explained importantly, then put it back. "It's not bad-tasting at all, sort of like brandy. He said it would fix me up right away, and it does — like magic. Oh, he's a doll, an absolute doll. He says it's not a bit serious, I just have to go very easy and take care of myself — and believe me, that's what I'm going to do."

Her air was suddenly so purposeful that Connie was moved to inquire, "How do you mean?"

"Well, I'm going to get a new car."

"What's wrong with yours? you've had it only three months."

"There's a new power-drive out," Myra explained, "where you hardly have to lift a finger. I'll get a wonderful trade-in on the old one, then I'll have a car that saves my strength." She smiled prettily at Connie. "I'm going to do a lot to the house, too."

"This house?"

"What other house have I?" Myra rallied her indulgently. "When my sweetie-doctor said I'd better cut down on climbing stairs, well, first I thought I'd move into an apartment – that new place in Orchard Estates – you know."

Connie did know; rents began there at three-fifty a month.

"But then I thought," Myra was saying, "I'm used to my poky little old house, so why not fix it up? put in a teeny elevator and a big beautiful powder-room downstairs, and all sorts of things. Ordinarily I wouldn't dream of spending the money, but when it's a question of health – being extravagant for your health is an economy," she explained, then giggled. "That kind of economy, that's for me. I'm going to have myself a time while I can still enjoy it. Archie was smart – he spent his money on himself. I'll be smart too." She looked straight at Connie with a smile, in which the malice was not completely overt. Connie shrugged, and Myra's smile became broader. She loved twisting the knife, and Connie's mental state was as clear to her as print — large print. Then, for the moment having satisfied her appetite for seeing her daughter-in-law squirm, "By the way," she added, "— about the funeral."

"What about it?" asked Connie, fully engaged in hanging onto her self-control. If Myra flaunted her prosperity in her face, only once more —!

"It's day after tomorrow, eleven o'clock, at the Mount Peace Chapel."

"I'm not going," said Connie promptly.

"Oh, you must, darling," Myra purred. "I won't have Ann go because she's got a cold, and I wouldn't like going alone. And only think how Archie treated me — kept me at a distance, wouldn't let me visit him at the san — well, I don't hold it against him." She preened again, this time virtuously. "I think, if that's the way he wanted it, all right — it's no time to bear malice, that's what I always say. I'll pick you up at ten-thirty, day after tomorrow," she finished conclusively. "That convertible of yours would strike a pretty gay note at a funeral."

"I want another drink," Connie announced, getting to her feet. When she returned from the sitting-room with her glass replenished, Myra appraised its much-deeper amber with a gleam of devilish comprehension.

"Whew!" she whistled softly. "Still, you need something to brace you, I daresay — with all this dull talk about estates and so forth." Myra had a genius — an unfailing, fiendish instinct — for touching the sore spot every time.

Connie's whole body shook inwardly with the spasm of her desire to slap Myra hard, right across that smile of hers, or dash the contents of her glass into her face — neither of which indulgences, alas, she dared grant herself. Instead, "Can you lend me some money?" she demanded, her voice abrupt and unsteady. She had not meant to do it so clumsily; Myra's damned needling always got to her.

"Money?" Myra's eyes widened innocently, as if hearing the word for the first time in her life. "Why do you need money?"

"I need it to live on," said Connie, ironic. "I'm flat — absolutely stony."

"But I don't understand why you *are* stony," Myra argued reasonably.

"You don't understand?" Connie repeated softly. "What with the big estate Bruce left me, of course I'm so *terribly* well-fixed."

"Whatever Bruce left, you got," said Myra. Her smile had vanished suddenly; over her face passed the faint constriction that still — after two years — manifested itself at any mention of her son's name. "You got all his insurance."

"All of fifteen thousand, two years ago," said Connie. "Funny, isn't it, that I'm not rolling?" She knew that this implied criticism of Bruce was a fatal mistake, yet some perverse instinct, combined with whisky, drove her on to dig her own grave.

"Do you expect me to support you?" queried Myra. "Why didn't you keep that money as a backlog, instead of just living on it? Most people never see fifteen thousand dollars in all their lives. You're able-bodied," she concluded. "Why don't you get a job?"

"Thanks," said Connie, "I wasn't brought up that way."

"Neither was Ann," Myra countered, "but Ann worked." Her smile was back again. "She didn't have to, God knows. The trouble with you, Connie, is that you're rotten conceited, and rotten lazy."

"I'm no lazier than you," said Connie, her voice tightening into harshness for a moment.

"Maybe not," Myra agreed amicably. "But you see I can afford to be lazy because I have the money, and you can't afford to be because you haven't. Simple?"

"I should think you'd want to help me, if only for Bruce's sake." Connie produced this argument with no great conviction as to its effectiveness, and her misgivings were confirmed in short order.

"Don't you dare give me that — for Bruce's sake!" Myra sat up straight, and a greenish glitter came into her eyes. "I loved him more than anyone on earth, and he knew it — which is more than he knew about you. Anyway," she added, "I *have* helped you — I've helped you lots of times."

"You've thrown me a few dollars here and there," Connie sneered recklessly, "for being your errand girl and running here and there doing all the dirty little jobs you don't want your precious Ann to do — like this morning."

A deathly dismay was seeping through Connie as she felt herself getting in deeper and deeper. She had not intended things to take this turn, much less to antagonize Myra by arguing with her. But she had had no lunch, and the second drink was swimming up into her head; the situation had slipped entirely beyond her control.

"I pay you well — too well — for the few trifling things you do for me," Myra was saying. "And believe me I do it for Brucie, not for you, but I'll think twice about how I do it in the future." She looked straight into Connie's eyes, and smiled once more. "You were married to him, all right," she finished softly, "but it's time you stopped trading on it."

Silence fell for several moments. Connie, carefully taking a sip of her drink, could feel the whiskey-heat stoking her pent-up rage and hatred.

"By the way," Myra resumed, "I understand that Jimmie Budd's been giving you a whirl. Why don't you marry him, if you're high and dry?"

"You marry Jimmy Budd," said Connie, very distinctly, "I don't like him."

"Beggars can't be choosers," caroled Myra, her habitual good-humor restored. Then she went off on another tangent; this was characteristic and showed that she had done with the subject in hand. "I'll have to dig out something black for the funeral, and I've very few black things," she said affably, as though they had been discussing clothes all along. "What a nuisance."

"How'll I live?" Connie broke out stridently. "What'll I do?"

Myra started to shrug, then arrested the shrug midway and reached for her bag. Taking a wallet from this – a bulging wallet – she counted out some bills and tossed them on the edge of the dressing-table nearest to Connie, saying, "There's a hundred, if you want it."

"A hundred," jeered Connie, making no move toward the money. "What good'll that do me?"

"Take it or don't take it," said Myra, with halcyon calm. "But I sort of think you will."

Connie was silent a moment; then, compressing her lips, and with a slanting glance at her mother-in-law, she slowly picked up the bills and shoved them into the pocket of her skirt. With all her soul she longed to rake Myra with a sample of the vitriol that always lay ready to her tongue, then follow it up by walking out for once and all; but her impecunious state was such that even this feeble resource must not be discarded too hastily or too finally.

"Don't look so ugly," Myra counseled sunnily. "It makes lines from your nose to your mouth, and believe me, pet, you can't afford that. – Oh, you're going?" For Connie had risen, first tripping slightly over her feet. "Well, thanks for going to the san and Luanna and all – and remember, I'm picking you up at ten-thirty day after tomorrow. Oh, by the way," she interpolated, "I've never been to the san, you know. Did that lawyer say if he kept anything important there — anything of value, I mean?"

"A watch and some cufflinks," shrugged Connie, walking carefully to the door. "Unless you want to count junk like clothes and books and a couple of desk-drawers full of diaries."

She had taken another step or two when a strange sound from Myra halted her; she turned, then stared incredulously. The familiar, youthful face beneath the red curls had vanished; a stranger's mask stared at her, an old woman's, haggard and distorted. As Connie stood rooted, surprised rather than concerned, Myra articulated thickly, "Bottle."

Connie stood weaving a little, slow on the uptake.

"Bottle," Myra got out once more. "Bag." An ugly stagnant flush darkened her face, her arms hung at her sides with a curious inertness, obviously with no power of motion. "Hurry."

Connie, recovering, hastily opened Myra's bag, found the bottle and unscrewed its top, placed the dropper between the old woman's lips. Myra sat motionless; after a few moments she said, "Another." Already her voice was perceptibly stronger. Connie redipped the glass rod into the bottle, and this time Myra was able to take it from her hand and place it between her own lips. In this position she remained unmoving, eyes closed, for a full couple of minutes at least.

The first flurry over, Connie observed her coolly as she sat there, breathing with slow, distinct expulsions of breath. Myra looked, for the first time in her daughter-in-law's experience, old and collapsed; her shoulders sagged, she seemed to have shrunk some degrees in size. However, she was plainly recovering; her color was becoming normal again.

"Feel better?" Connie ventured.

"I'm all right," said Myra. She still had that crushed, leaden look, her eyes were still closed, but her voice was clear and curt. "You go on now."

Connie turned toward the door, and once again checked, visited by a most unfortunate inspiration — but her power of judgment was clouded, first by alcohol, secondly by Myra's suddenly-withered, feeble look.

"Myra," she wheedled, "I'm up a tree, really — couldn't you spare me another couple of hundred? just until —"

Mrya's eyes shot open, and glared straight into Connie's.

"Stop hounding me for money!" she screamed, with unexpected strength. "Aren't you ashamed when I'm like this, aren't you ashamed —" Her voice failed; she began to move her head from side to side distressfully, while her arms made flailing gestures which Connie interpreted as motioning her toward the door. Nothing loath, she escaped from the room, and stood in the hall for a moment, pondering Myra's violent outcry in a state of foggy astonishment. This had time to evaporate during her careful negotiation of the stairs; when she reached bottom, all her earlier corroding anxiety and resentment were again churning in her, full force. What she needed now was some object on which to vent them — an object she found in the girl who moved forward to meet her from the dimmer reaches of the hall. This was Ann Walworth, Myra's daughter, by five or six years Connie's junior.

CHAPTER 6

A curious atmosphere instantly made itself felt in the hall as the one girl approached the other. Connie could remember no time when Ann had not roused in her anything but different degrees of dislike, varied by contempt for the fool who had gone to work – as soon as she graduated college – as a laboratory technician. All that money behind her, yet choosing to work as paid help, like a stenographer or a salesgirl or something; only affectation or plain stupidity, in Connie's book, could account for behaviour so perverse. Now, watching with suddenly narrowed eyes as her sister-in-law came on, a churning brew of resentment, malice and spite boiled up to a head suddenly. The smug little bitch, lucky, safe, warmly swathed in security – and she, Connie, cringing from the cold breath on her neck, the breath of that world which was so implacable to the moneyless! In particular she had always been galled by Ann's peculiarly clear look, direct and comprehensive, as well as by the youthful contour of her cheeks and the clarity of her brow, all of which combined to make her look younger than her age — and, by implication, made Connie feel that much older. Especially Connie hated what she called "that damned *look* of hers," not knowing that this high, collected air of Ann's was the direct result of the bracing process, the summoning of courage, that she must always put herself through, like a drill, at the prospect of any encounter with her sister-in-law. Why Connie should affect her so strongly and unpleasantly, and why this feeling should not abate at all with the passage of time, she could not have said; the causes underlay reason, originating somewhere in instinct. At this moment, still some feet away, she caught a potent whiff of alcohol from the motionless, ominously-waiting figure, and cautioned herself to walk accordingly.

"Hello, Connie," she began, in a voice rendered husky by a slight sore throat. Then, in the dimness, she took in Connie's aspect and baleful eyes, and understood that she could dispense with the amenities. "What happened upstairs?" she went on. "I could hear Mamma from down here. — What happened?" she urged again, with increasing nervousness.

Connie reminded her of an animal about to spring, with that flattened look about her head, and that silence.

"What happened," said Connie after a further interval, and with exaggerated distinctness, "happens to be none of your God-damned business."

"It happens to be my business," retorted Ann, "because she happens to be my mother." She was angry, and it felt good; it made her forget her policy of restraint and her shrinking nerves. "The one thing she can't stand right now is being worried or upset, on account of her heart. She can't stand it, do you hear? So either keep the peace, or stay away from her. If you've got to start arguments with her, just don't come around, that's all."

"So?" Connie almost purred. Her face had gone a curious dusky white, her eyes were half-shut; in one corner of her mouth shone a bubble of saliva. "Who're you, anyway? Is this your house? you think I'll stay away on your sayso?"

"I think you'll do just exactly that," said Ann coolly, but in a lowered voice, glancing anxiously toward the stairs.

"Will I? and if I want to come, who'll keep me away?"

"I will —"

Ann broke off in total disgust — with herself more than with Connie; she had handled it as badly as possible, after all her self-admonition. "Look, Connie, don't let's brawl," she said rapidly. "Come on, let's talk outside. I'm not trying to throw my weight around — I just want you to understand about Mamma. Let's go outside."

"Oh, drop dead, you —" Connie let loose a string of surprising expressions, her voice a monotone, almost inaudible; the bubble at the corner of her mouth had brought forth several young, and the cluster slid and winked with the motion of her lips.

"You're drunk," said Ann less disturbed than might have been expected at the remarkable specimen of gutter eloquence. Connie was hardly ever far gone in liquor, but on such occasions was invariably foul-mouthed. "And you'd better lie down here and sleep it off," Ann continued. "You'll kill someone if you go out and drive when you're like that."

"How," inquired Connie, forming each syllable with great meticulousness, "how would you like to have that face of yours slapped?"

"Oh, go home." Ann shrugged, half-turned away. "But you'd better sleep it off somewhere, if not here —"

She interrupted herself again. Beneath

Connie's insolence there was borne to her, on some current of intuition, a fever-beat of despair, and she felt a momentary concern, almost pity. "Look, Connie," she said urgently. "was the trouble between Mamma and you money? because if it was, I can let you have some — I need hardly any, living here. From now on come to me instead of Mamma, won't you? I can always give you a little —"

"A little," Connie broke in softly. "God, are you true to type — cheap like your mother, like all your family, cheap as dirt. Keep your buck, I'm not down to that yet. Keep it and —" she concluded with another noisome injunction and walked out, letting the door bang back unlatched. Ann secured it, looking after Connie until she vanished around the corner of the house, moving with exaggerated circumspection. Then she stood for some moments in the hall, listening; no sound came from upstairs. Feeling the moment unpropitious for inquiries, she withdrew slowly to her own room, closed the door, and stood reflective.

Her room was somewhat disheveled, a place of comfort and excessive warmth; she loved this hideaway on the ground floor with its catticorner fireplace, which she kept burning all day, from the first of Autumn coolness straight through the Winter. To sit baking in that glow, while inattentively waterlogging her mind with miscellaneous reading, supplied her great present need – an antidote against thought. The warmth was protective, lulling and narcotic; it dulled – intermittently at least – the gnawing within her, the wild ache of postponement. Often, in a sort of wonderment, she recalled her life of only four years ago, the job that she had filled so capably, with such an uplifting sense of being in her right niche, doing what she ought to do. A rapid clear stream that life seemed to her now, running along with the power of purpose, destination. By what disastrous chance had it trickled out in this backwater, this muddy, stagnant puddle? The first fatal misstep, she was well aware, had been the giving up of her job and coming to live at home again, on the occasion of her brother's death and Myra's immediate collapse. She realized this too late, but at the time it had seemed imperative, unavoidable – what with the extent and nature of Myra's break-up; her reaction at being left a widow had been negligible by comparison. This had been the origin of Myra's present hold on her – a hold that never slackened, but renewed and reinforced itself in various ways, some blatant, some subtle – tentacle after tentacle settling into place and tightening. And when the passage of time finally brought her to a pitch desperate enough to attempt breaking away from that multiple constraint – then Myra had fallen ill again. Not seriously, but genuinely ill. Now, as in a crystal ball, Ann had an accurate vision of her future; every time she would try to leave, Myra would have a heart-attack. She loved her mother, but could estimate her dispassionately – her trickiness, her large and varied repertory of tactics, single-mindedly used for the purpose of getting her own way.

I'm cooked, was Ann's most frequent assurance to herself these days; I'm trapped. And seeing this prospect before her, indefinitely protracted; feeling the corrosion of idleness, knowing her hard-won professional skills rusting, slipping away from her, she had moments of black panic. Trembling, she would steady herself with the same words repeated again and again, like an incantation. *I'm myself,* she would asseverate silently, not always with belief. *I won't become someone else. I won't become a worse person. I won't become nothing.* This device had worked up till now; always, if she talked to herself long enough, the black wave would recede.

Then, on top of her stagnant life in this silent, overheated room, another misfortune, and worse, had overtaken her; she had fallen in love with Dr. Markham. At once her weight of trouble submerged beneath a new weight, a pain such as she had never before experienced and could hardly have imagined. When he visited Myra, she contrived to encounter him in the hall, with a humiliating sense that he was aware of her tactics, and an added sense — still more humiliating — that they were unwelcome to him. Sometimes brusquely, sometimes remotely, he continued to overlook her; she realized that he was engrossed in some problem or trouble, and that his degree of insulation was proof against any assault she could make. After awhile his continuing denial of her — of her presence — crushed the hope out of her and turned her heart to lead. She had insane impulses to yell at him: *look at me, look at me and see me. Do that much, won't you? do that much for me, just once?* Then she began revolving ways and means, pretexts for going to see him at his office — perhaps about Myra? surely that would look natural, about her mother . . .? She would invent and reject expedients until she was dizzy and had to let up, but there was no let-up in her fainting need to see him, hear him . . . she tried to visualize him now, as an antidote to the horrid scene just past. But over his image was superimposed a stronger, more recent one, that she could not shake from her mind. Always she remembered – with incredulity – the nature and extent of the fascination that Connie had had for her brother. What ailed Bruce, that he could go overboard in such a manner for such a creature . . .? And yet – for she had a rigid sense of fairness – it might be that much of her aversion was mere jealousy; if she were a man, perhaps she would find Connie fascinating too, with that marvelous figure, that clear pale skin, those long, long lashes. Except that all these attractive separate parts added up to something so unpleasantly disconcerting, disturbing . . . and again, all this might be merely her individual reaction.

Then suddenly – with alarming clarity – she heard her mother's outcry of a few minutes ago; that strident voice, barely recognizable. Myra, the soul of smiling self-possession (except for the one episode of her son's death); how could Connie, of all people, manage to force from her that tormented scream?

Ann frowned, then rubbed at the frown, automatically. From nowhere a shiver took her; a vague sense of impending misfortune. But she could only wait – wait to see what might come of the episode, then grapple with Connie, if necessary . . . the thought inspired, to her own surprise, something very like fear. To come to grips with that unknown quantity – yes, unknown; she felt suddenly that Connie was almost a complete mystery to her.

All this time she had been staring toward a shadowy corner of the room, unseeing; now, as she moved, an image in the corner moved, too. Startled, then realizing, she looked toward the mirror with sudden awareness, and saw a girl with a burdened, indeterminate look, a *quenched* look . . . quickly she raised her chin and threw her shoulders back. Easy to let one's self go, so easy, she thought, comparing her crumpled, ungroomed look with Connie's elegant slimness.

"You needn't let down all the way," she exhorted herself, with contempt. Angrily she snatched up a comb and drove it through her thick chestnut hair, attacking it like an enemy.

"Brucie," muttered Connie, muzzily heading for her car, "Mamma's boy." In these terms she thought of her young husband, dead four years – when not mentally execrating him for having cheated her. For this was what he had done, it was the long and short of it; letting her marry him on the assumption that his mother had millions and would do handsomely by them.

She climbed into her car and headed for home, a superb driver drunk or sober, presently turning a private lane on a country road and stopping before a small gatehouse, which she had at a nominal rental from Lydia Hussey; one of her few pieces of luck in this lean period. Here she got out, and walked up to the main house — a sprawling old place in bad repair, fragile and ramshackle, where Lydia lived and bred miniature Poms.

In the vast living-room, as Connie entered, no fewer than eighteen or twenty little dogs disported themselves on their various occasions, excluding none; the room twitched in every part with perpetual motion, like tic. Enthroned in this flea-like animation Lydia sat at ease in a big leather chair, her back against one arm-piece, her legs slung over the other, and a glass in her hand. A big rangy woman with pepper-and-salt hair, weatherbeaten complexion and a whisky voice, she was dressed in cotton shirt and bluejeans — her invariable uniform except when exhibiting dogs. On these occasions she would reluctantly get some sort of permanent, enamel her work-worn nails cerise, and truss herself with the unfamiliar confines of a bra, girdle and dress.

Connie came forward without a greeting and with perfect aplomb, knowing with whom she had to deal, and made a beeline toward the bottle and ice that stood on the portable bar. Lydia watched her sourly, in silence; only the sound of the whisky gurgling into the glass roused her to speech.

"Use up my liquor, that's right," she remarked without heat. "Three months' rent you owe me, and lap up my whisky into the bargain."

Connie, splashing in soda, ignored her.

"Everything going out, nothing coming in," Lydia went on. "The dam' dogs keep breeding, three litters so far this month, and I haven't made a Goddamned sale in two weeks. Who'll keep us?" she demanded severely of a tiny female (pregnant) who, as if in answer, commenced a number of heavings incredibly subterranean considering her size, and presently laid all on the carpet, then gazed up at Lydia with melting eyes and an expression of conscious virtue.

"Oh hell," said Lydia mildly, veiled the scene with a newspaper, and inquired fondly, "Feel better, angel?" Without pause she returned her attention to Connie, inquiring, "How's about a check? Three months' rent, a hundred and twenty. Or any part of it. I could use it, b'lieve me — how 'bout it?"

"Tomorrow," said Connie, and escaped from

the shabby, smelly room, carrying a tall drink that was about one-half whisky. She was not a hard drinker, in fact she disapproved of Lydia's habitual drunkenness from 6 P.M. onward, but the day had been hellish; she had to obliterate herself, knock herself out; every nerve in her body cried for oblivion. This drink, added to what she had had at Myra's, should do it.

Once in her house she went up directly to her bedroom, ripped off her clothes down to her lingerie, kicked off her shoes, and emptied the glass avidly, with a sort of desperate ardor, bending her head far back for the last drop. This done, she staggered slightly and recovered herself, while a vague impression assailed her; that something odd had happened in connection with Myra, something she ought to pin down and think about. For a few seconds she stayed on her feet, grappling unsteadily with the problem, to no effect. Then the drink hit her; she dropped on the bed, dead weight, and fell like a stone into the lightless depths, the unrelieved black night she craved so greedily.

CHAPTER 7

Connie woke around noon, and got up at once. She felt little the worse for drinking; the real hangover was her recollection of the previous day, with its horrible, bruising succession of disasters.

She went downstairs, put on coffee, waited for it restlessly while roaming about without purpose, gnawed and fretted by worry. That was the failure of drinking where she was concerned; instead of releasing her from a sense of her troubles, it was likely to underline and deepen it — which was why, in general, she had little recourse to liquor. Archie, the filthy old sneak, letting her down over the bequest; Myra, dam' her, twitting her with her poverty, flinging her that pittance; Ann, so *very* kindly offering her own two cents . . . jerkily, her nerves plucked raw with her resentments, she moved about, hung up her jacket, decided that the coffee would take forever coming to the boil, and went upstairs. Here she started picking up her flung-about clothes, then remembered Myra's dole and took it from her skirt-pocket — a handful of crumpled bills. She straightened them out, mentally earmarking a twenty for Lydia, to shut her up for awhile. Her wallet was in her bag; she opened it, groped without looking among the familiar contents, withdrew the wallet. But it was not a wallet. She looked at it blankly a moment, with complete and genuine non-recognition, before identifying it for what it was — Archie's diary. Absolutely no memory of putting it in her bag remained to her. At this moment, from downstairs, came the virulent hiss of the coffee boiling over, and she descended hastily, the diary still in her hand.

Ten minutes later Connie sat at the little table near the window, her second cup of black coffee before her. She felt much more awake, and was afraid; being awake meant that she would begin to think. Lighting a cigarette, she let it burn untouched upon her saucer, and sat empty-eyed, inert; from time to time a faint frown twitched between her brows. Past her effort of will to hold herself mindless, the bleak problems started moving in: the absolute necessity for finding work of some kind, the prospect of being questioned about her non-existent qualifications, the certainty of being rejected by people she would not have bothered (in her own words) to spit on. She took a fresh grip on her intention not to think; if she began to think, she would begin to despair.

Without interest, only to keep thought at bay, she took up the diary, riffled its pages, read one or two jottings at random.

June 6. Still lovely weather. This is not important to me any more; sun does not cheer me, rain does not depress me. The aspects of the world have little interest for one no longer of it, for I feel the world receding from me, or rather, I feel myself receding from the world. — This afternoon collected a foursome for bridge and managed to last one rubber. Small loss; Mrs. C. a horrible player and the others mediocre. T.D. July 22. Hardly able to eat; the food well-prepared and delicious (I suppose) but it tastes like sawdust and lies heavy as lead. I consider this total loss of appetite a major downward step; Dr. B. says not. Liar.

July 28. Tried to read, first Arabia Deserta, then Massingham's English Downland, both of which in their different ways have given me exquisite pleasure; hardly able to take in the meaning of the simplest sentences. This suggests to me: what enormous, taken-for-granted complexity in one phrase, one word, of our daily language!

Simple while one can use it, unattainably difficult when one cannot. T.D.

Aug. 3. T.D.

At this point Connie, incredibly bored, nevertheless experienced a faint twinge of curiosity. Those two capital letters (she riffled the pages again) appearing so frequently, sometimes standing alone under the date: what was their significance? In a younger person she would unhesitatingly read one meaning into them, an affair (only *quite* so often?) but for an old and dying man, the explanation must be otherwise. Half-interested, she began leafing the diary, page by page, and finally stopped where a much longer entry caught her eye; the writing was spidery and tremulous, sometimes wavering off into illegibility.

Sept 8. An unusually good night, sound sleep; I woke at five and congratulated myself; it was one time that I had escaped T.D. A premature conclusion, it seems, for I fell asleep once more, and at once — there it was, as so often, so tormentingly often: The Dream. Incredible how it never fades, nor expands, nor contracts; no, it remains the same, every hateful detail sharp; distinctly, painfully sharp. Once more I am standing before a closed door in the long upstairs hall; toward its end I can just see the marble heads of that idiotic group on the landing. (Father gave $2700 for it, I *remember.) The house is quiet, dead quiet; and behind the door, too, everything is quiet. This is the horror, for I could stop what is going on behind that door, and I do not stop it. I am letting it happen; more than that, I am assisting, lending myself to it, for I am stationed there as a lookout, to give warning if anyone comes up. But no one comes, no one at all.*

Then I hear a sound behind the door; at this point in The Dream, my heart beats suffocatingly. The door opens, and M. comes out. And I know that it is done. Not by what means, however; for she has nothing in her hands, she looks cool, collected, her hair is undisturbed and her dress unmussed (as in fact they did look) which must mean that there has been no violence.

So far TD has followed, with complete fidelity, the real sequence of events (as if a film of it had been taken on the spot and were being run off for my exclusive benefit almost every night) but now, at this point, it begins to diverge from actuality. M. has come out of the bedroom; we stand looking at each other. Suddenly there is a sound — horrors, a footstep; a slow, deliberate footstep in the empty house. Someone is coming upstairs. We stand paralyzed, staring; I can see that she is as horrified as myself. The person, whoever it is, reaches the landing, starts ascending the remaining steps; I can see the top of his head —

his or hers, I am never sure which, because at this point I always wake with a frightful start. But this part is infinitely more oppressive than the rest — which is odd, because in reality, of course, there were no footsteps. M. simply came out of the bedroom looking calm and unruffled, and we went downstairs and waited for the other two and for the nurse. And that is TD, over and over again, without one single modification or variation. I daresay if, out of curiosity, I compared this note with my first written account of TD, eleven years ago, I would find the two identical in every particular. Am tired now, must stop.

Then, a half-inch below, in a very pale hand that fell about in all directions: *How did she do it? have never stopped asking myself that question. Will probably never know. — Do the others dream, I wonder. Most likely not.*

This was the final entry — September eighth. He had died day before yesterday . . . what was today? — he had died October 28th.

Connie leaned back from her perusal of the diary, and for some moments sat perfectly still. A bar of color had appeared along her cheekbones; her eyes, intent and unpleasantly bright, were fixed on a point beyond the room. Deep within her had begun a hum of excitement, a burring as of a dynamo starting up, and though she tried to suppress this as premature, yet its vibration continued to shake her slightly and shorten her breathing. Had she stumbled upon something or not?

Once more she read the entry; as she finished, a chilling thought fell on her like a blight. Could it all be invention on Archie's part, merely some straying fantasy of his illness? It was entirely possible . . . suddenly her heart leaped with excitement. The nurse at the san had mentioned nightmares, surely? Of course! *They wore him out a good deal,* she had said, or words to that effect. So it was no mere invention; he had really dreamed – presumably of something that had actually happened. What it was, of course, she could not quite tell from this one entry. But apparently Archie and Myra – *M.* could mean no one but Myra – had been up to something together, and this something had taken place in the old Gedney house, now Luanna's; the allusion to the statue on the landing made it unmistakable to anyone previously acquainted with the place. Then, the next consideration: what was the actual deed in which her mother- and uncle-in-law had been associated? "Eleven years ago." to quote Archie's own words; eleven years ago she had not yet married into the Gedney family, it was all before her time. If she wanted to find out anything, some digging into the Gedney annals was indicated — cautious digging. Eleven years was a long time, but not impossibly or hopelessly long.

Again she started reading the diary from the very beginning, in hope of additional information. This failed to materialize, and yet her feeling — that she was on the trail of something — took hold of her with a renewed grip. By nature she was as clever as she was lazy; her deepest instincts were predatory; her need for money made her tigerish. Her agile mind, in fact, had instantly flown to an expert on Gedney history, a talking archive, inexhaustible — but was it safe to tap this source? If any rumor of her inquiries should find their way back to Myra . . . but this was highly improbable, considering the paucity of Myra's connection with Luanna's household. Connie was always her emissary to the old Gedney ark whenever necessity arose, for Myra had an ingrained loathing of sickroom visits and old age. Therefore, it should be safe enough to pump Mrs. Donlan; you couldn't hold out for a hundred percent safety in anything . . . she lifted the phone.

When Mrs. Donlan answered, she greeted her affably, inquired after Luanna, ostensibly at Myra's instance, and let Mrs. Donlan gab away; she would go on forever, once you got her started. Connie allowed her a sufficient warming-up period, then deemed it safe to say, "Mrs. Donlan, do you remember anything special happening in the family, eleven years ago? I've made a bet with someone — about a date. You would know about it, if anyone did," she asked flatteringly. "I said to myself, Mrs. Donlan's the one to ask, she knows more about the Gedneys than they do themselves."

"Well, I do, a'most, but —" Mrs. Donlan fell silent for a moment; then, " 'Leven years ago?" she repeated, ruminatively. "Somethin' special happened in the family?"

"According to my information, yes."

"But what happened? what kind o' thing?"

"That's what you'll tell me," said Connie. "That's the bet."

"Where'd it happen?"

"In your house," said Connie. "Where you work."

"Are you sure —" Mrs. Donlan's voice was more and more uncertain, "— it was eleven years ago?"

"That's my information — that's what I've bet on."

"Well then," stated Mrs. Donlan, decisively, "I can't help you. There's nothin' happened in this house 'leven years ago, an I'll take my oath on that."

84

"How can you be so sure?" protested Connie, with the first faint sinking of dismay.

"I'll tell you how," responded Mrs. Donlan. "I can place it exact, by when Aggie came to work here. I been here thirty-two years, an' she's been here goin' on twelve; an' nothin's happened a-tall since Aggie came to work for Miss Luanna."

Connie was silent and sick; had Archie, after all, led her up the garden path? Through her dismay, Mrs. Donlan's voice penetrated once more. "— Aggie," she was saying. "entered Miss Lu's *im*-ploy right after Mrs. Gedney died. But that wasn't eleven years ago," she concluded doubtfully. "It's nearer twelve. It ain't her you'd be meanin', is it?"

"No —" she had begun answering mechanically, when in delayed reaction a thrill shot along her nerves; had Mrs. Donlan supplied the answer after all, and she not realized it? "No," she repeated, trying to keep the excitement out of her voice. "Well, I've made a mistake and lost a bet, that's all."

She ended the conversation quickly, hanging up with a curious reflective gentleness; then sat for quite an interval, tranced with speculation. She had never known old Mrs. Gedney, step-mother of Myra and Archie and the rest of them, but Bruce had mentioned her at some

85

time or other; it was at this old lady's death that the Gedney estate had finally been broken up among the four brothers and sisters — that estate whose size she had so greviously over-estimated when she had married the slender, rather delicate Bruce. That drip, her mind flung at him now, before reverting to more crucial matters. Well, then, it must be Mrs. Gedney's death that Archie referred to in his diary; the death of their stepmother. And if her conjecture were true, she had to hand it to them; among themselves they had cooked up something so good that it held water until the present day. There had never been a breath of suspicion, let alone of accusation; if there had been such an episode in the family, she was bound to have heard of it. Still, all this was nothing but theory, and a moment of leaden discouragement fell upon her. To raise a twelve-year-old murder — if there had been a murder at all — out of its grave; to dig up corroboration that was damning enough, solid and intimidating enough, to serve as a weapon in the campaign of blackmail she already envisaged . . . no, it was hopeless, impossible. This conviction engulfed her in a still deeper despondency, from which she could barely emerge. Still, she reminded herself, she might as well see what she could do; in fact, she had no choice, what with the stark desperation of her circumstances; she must try, she had nothing to lose. And even this early in her activities, one thing was clear in her mind; they had killed the old lady for money. It had to be so; it was the only reason that made sense. Native to Connie's mind was the cold conviction that money was the one thing worth killing for.

Well, now she had her motive, or her theory of a motive, rather; the next step was to confirm it, if possible. Where had she heard — somewhere or other — that wills were public documents and could be consulted at pleasure by anyone?

The courthouse at Hargesville, the county-seat, was an ugly old monster in portentous red brick, a post-Civil War architectural abortion. Vast wooden staircases threaded it with echoes from top to bottom; its high corridors, where the bare boards were slick beneath the foot, were full of the slight degraded stink of all public buildings, a composite of old disinfectant, mouldering nests of rags in broom-closets, old cigarette-odor, body-odor. Before the old-fashioned door whose diamond-glass panel announced in black letters, REGISTRAR OF WILLS, Connie paused a moment, then turned the knob and went in.

It was a medium-sized room filled with desks, which were separated from the public by a counter and a metal grill. In a further wall, the door of a vault stood open. A middle-aged woman rose in lackadaisical fashion from the nearest desk and came forward; considerably nervous beneath her composed, aloof air, Connie began, "I'd like to see a will —" but there was no need for nervousness at all; bored, unquestioning, the woman made a note of the year, 1923, and the name, Chester Hoskinson Gedney, and vanished through the door of the vault. Connie's ready command of this information was derived from a quick visit to the family plot an hour ago, and there it was, sprawled pompously all over a huge shaft of polished granite, buttressed by the names of his two wives, Adeline and Margaret, on a lower line, and in meeker lettering. Connie had hardly glanced at her husband's grave, on which was lying a large floral piece, very fresh. At the entrance to the plot a handsome metal marker stuck in the ground announced: PERPETUAL CARE.

The attendant reappeared, bearing a sort of box — one of those legal affairs in tan leatherette and black marbleized cardboard. From this she extracted a document in a blue cover, and handed it to Connie — who, surprised at its thickness said, "Is there any place I can sit down and look at this?"

"You can look at it here," said the woman, with standard public-employee indifference, and indicated the counter.

"It's a quarter-inch thick," snapped Connie, her brand of unpleasantness more than a match for the drab clerk's. "Do you expect me to go through this standing on my feet?"

The woman started to reply, but "Miss Mumbauer," a man's voice broke in dismissively; he had risen from a desk beside a window and was approaching them. "Can I help you?" he asked pleasantly. Connie explained, and he said at once, "Come in, come in," and buzzed the door of the grill. She stepped through into the enclosure with the desks, and he conducted her through the door of the vault. Within this, enclosed by serried ranks of book-case-looking structures up to the dark ceiling, stood a heavy oblong table with chairs around it, in which a couple of men were already seated.

"It's a little more comfortable here," said her guide.

"Not much, for the taxes we pay," Connie responded coldly; he vanished as if rebuked, and Connie ensconced herself, noting that her companions, from some remark one made to the other, seemed to be lawyers. Then she opened the formidable sheaf, and settled herself to read.

Twenty pages and ten minutes later, her head swimming, she was no wiser than when she had begun. Those dense paragraphs of legal phraseology, those interminable lists of holdings, of property real and personal, the complicated, technical instructions regarding their disposition; most of it was incomprehensible, all of it unbelievably dull. Still, she must plow through it to the last word; she dare not leave any part of it unread. The light was poor and she was unaccustomed to concentrating at any length. The close, dusty smell of the vault, along with the indigestible reading matter, began pressing her into a stupor of boredom; her eyes and her attention clouded, she yawned, almost nodded . . . all at once she sat up straight, nudged into renewed alertness. This paragraph, on next to the last page — this one short paragraph . . . bored no longer, she read and re-read it, devoured it, while conviction crystallized within her; this must be it, and if considered attentively, was motive enough for a dozen murders. Borne on a sudden upsurge of encouragement and energy, she rose and left the vault, actually calling a brief, "Thank you" to the man at his desk. An inward paean of triumph accompanied her on her progress out of the smelly old barrack. Reading that will was like boring through a tough protective shell, but she had gotten to the nut at last.

In her livingroom, she seized upon the diary, quickly devoured the significant entry. This time, another phrase — hitherto unnoticed — struck its prongs deep into her attention; a bare allusion, unexplained. But surely it seemed to indicate that, beside Myra and Archie, others were involved? . . . She fastened upon the lines, re-read them.

Myra simply came out of the bedroom looking calm and unruffled, and we went downstairs and waited for the other two and for the nurse. Who could *the other two* be, her common sense informed her, but Luanna and Theo?

We . . . waited for the other two. . . .

Where had Luanna and Theo been, while Myra and Archie were upstairs? But in any case, one thing seemed sure; that all four of the Gedney inheritors had gotten together on a plan for accelerating the death of their stepmother, and the reason why was abundantly supplied by that single paragraph in their father's will.

. . . we waited for the other two, and for the nurse . . .

Had the nurse been implicated too? as an assistant? an accomplice? She wished she could get hold of that nurse. Mrs. Donlan would probably remember the woman's name, but to call her again so soon, and with so peculiar a question . . . then suppose Mrs. Donlan to mention these inquiries to Myra; Connie gave her head a brief, emphatic shake in the negative, discarding Mrs. Donlan from her procedure. She must get the nurse's name some other way — but how?

And then, suddenly —

"My God," said Connie, as if blinded by revelation. She snatched up the phone, gave a number; while waiting for it, "You fool, you fool," she excoriated herself, "how can you be such a fool?" Here she was, fumbling in the dark, trying to reconstruct the thing by guess — when waiting for her was a gold-mine, a cache of information straight from the horse's mouth! In imagination she stood once more in Archie's room at the sanitarium; once more she looked down into a desk-drawer full of neatly-stacked journals. What might they not contain? names, dates, plans, perhaps an account of the — the murder itself. (Connie was momentarily jolted as she realized that this was the word for it.) But in those diaries, if anywhere, was evidence — detailed, incriminating; a precious lode of the raw material of blackmail, complete — for judging from the entries she had seen, it was Archie's old-fashioned habit to confide everything to his journal.

The ringing signal had begun; a voice answered with the name of the sanitarium. Connie asked for Miss Selden, who came on the phone after a slight delay. Connie identified herself, and was at once aware that Miss Selden's manner had changed utterly from her manner of yesterday, and that her voice, by some occult inflection, managed to combine perfect courtesy with freezing contempt. The episode of the gardener's children had gotten back to her, of course; not that it really mattered.

"Miss Selden," said Connie, going at once to the point, "I told Mrs. Walworth about her brother's leaving all those diaries, you know? and she'd prefer to have them as soon as possible; she doesn't like the idea of personal papers lying around like that. Mr. Sinclair even asked me to take them before the things were appraised — you could check with him on that, if you like. They're of no money value, of course — so would there be any objection to my coming over and getting them? now?"

"There'd be no objection as far as I'm concerned," returned Miss Selden glacially, "except that they're not here any more. Mrs. Walworth came over and took the diaries, quite early this morning."

CHAPTER 8

Half-past five and late afternoon light, melancholy, of the shortening days of Autumn. At this hour Ralph Markham's discontents caught up with him, full impact and full weight. He sat now before his desk in the fatigue of after-office hours, his legs straight out, his shoulders a little slumped. The building — a remodeled house containing three doctors' offices — was empty; the secretary and the two nurses, employees of the three jointly, had gone. The air was full of silence, the very faint smell of the heating-system, and a composite, not-unpleasant medical odor.

He felt done-up, exhausted; yet irritable and restless. As always at this time of day, he began thinking of Linda, of their broken engagement (but more from habit now than from any active pain); for the thousandth time speculating as to the likelihood of her throwing him over later for something else, if she had not thrown him over sooner about that Laboratory Station affair. He had had a midsummer invitation, of long standing, to spend a couple of weeks at the beautiful country home that she and her parents occupied from May to October; by the malice of fate, he had received the offer – perfectly unexpected – of a whole month's work at the Woods Hole Experimental Station, the month taking in two weeks promised to Linda. The opportunity was not to be passed up; every doctor and scientist tried to get into the Station at some period or other of his working life. After a couple of embattled sessions (telephonic) with Linda, he had gone off to the Station. And in spite of the consequences, he could hardly regret that month even now; the marvelous, perfectly unique field of research made possible by the wealth of marine life brought up, every day, in the Station's nets. Some of these (though this was not a prime consideration) were unknown and unclassified, and one day the catch had even included – miracle of miracles – a synapta. Miraculous because the synapta was a denizen of southern-most tropic seas, and by what aberration of sub-ocean currents it had appeared so far north could only be regarded as a mystery. Still, the summer had been torrid, and the ocean, day after day, like warm milk. In appearance this creature was the very stuff of nightmare — a huge seaworm, about eight feet long and three or four inches wide. Its head, eyeless, resembled nothing so much as a cluster of furry fingers; each finger, with apparently unlimited powers of contraction and expansion, could work its way into cracks and crevices hardly visible to the eye — and did, in its obscene, blind, never-ending quest for food. — Well, the Woods Hole interim had been a first-rate professional experience, invaluable; then he had come home and found himself minus a fiancée.

Aftermaths, he reflected moodily, were unavoidable, after any amputation. With irritation he switched off the brilliant desk-light and sat in the dusk, trying, also for the thousandth time, to decide whether he were still in love with Linda. Probably he was getting over her; he might as well sooner as later. And a good thing too, for — of all the girls in the world — she was probably the worst bet for a doctor's wife. But all at once she was vividly before him, in all the perfection of her youth and her honey-blondness; spoiled, avid for nothing but pleasure and amusement and luxury, but bright and vivacious . . . and lovely, so lovely and graceful . . . he shook his head abruptly as though shaking her from his mind, and sat for a few minutes, carefully blank.

Then, deliberately — as a counter-irritant — he began thinking of Connie Walworth. The slender waist, the sinuousness of her body when she moved, her faintly reckless and libertine air . . . jerking on the light, he fished for the telephone book. The empty evening would be no worse for dinner and bed with this upper-class tramp. And if the whole thing were mere stop-gap, debased — well, he was cheating no one but himself.

The book disclosed only one Walworth, Myra, and he knew her household well enough to be positively certain that Connie's address and hers were not the same. And it would be impossibly awkward to call Mrs. Myra and ask for Mrs. Connie's phone number, and how else to trace it he had no idea, except . . . a bout with local Information elicited the expected answer; the operator could offer him no Walworth except Myra. When he rejected her, she was extremely firm about no Mrs. Connie being listed. Of course, for all he knew, she might live nowhere near this locality; he had assumed it, that was all.

As a matter of fact, Connie, under stress of hard times, had delayed having a phone put in, and made free use of Lydia's, not excluding toll calls. If she could have realized, this evening, the consequences of her non-appearance in the book, her regret would have rendered pale by comparison that of her would-be playmate.

He sailed the book back onto its shelf, and resumed staring glumly into space. Then the phone rang. Unmoving, he sat looking at it. A patient ringing, of course; who else? But suppose it were Connie Walworth . . . between scepticism and excitement he lifted the receiver, and said in a neutral voice, "Dr. Markham speaking."

Someone uttered something indistinctly; he frowned and said, "I can't hear you. Who is it, please?"

The voice raised itself with, as it seemed, a maximum of effort; achieved audibility. "This is Ann Walworth, Dr. Markham – Ann Walworth."

"Oh, yes, Miss Walworth." He waited; nothing followed but a dead silence. "Yes, Miss Walworth?" he repeated, between impatience and perplexity. "What is it, any trouble? your mother?"

"No, not my mother." She was speaking in an odd manner – brokenly, with curious failures of breath. "I – I wanted – I mean –" She stopped again.

"Yes?" he said coldly, with ironic resignation, now certain that her call was a pretext, for he was by no means oblivious of the meetings she contrived. For coping with the doctor's chief occupational hazard – unwelcome female advances – he was as well-equipped as the next; yet, since this particular female was so very young, a mere girl, he only demanded, "Just what did you want, Miss Walworth?" His sardonic patience was effective; seeming not only to steady her, but to produce in her own voice an answering note of coolness.

"I'd like to know your office-hours," she said, distinctly now, "in case I had to see you away from the house."

"My office-hours," he informed her, "are from three-thirty to five-thirty every day except Saturdays and Sundays." But, finding himself somewhat puzzled, "You don't want to come around now?"

"No!" She seemed to retreat from this suggestion precipitately, as if in panic. "I just wanted to know when to find you – in case I had to come."

"About yourself?" What was she getting at, or did she herself know?

"No – not about myself."

"About your mother then?" he persisted, more and more nonplussed.

"Well –" she said evasively; then with a rush, "But I may not have to come at all –

thank you, doctor," and hung up.

He followed suit more slowly, and sat for a moment musing sourly on the perverseness of fate; it would have to be, of course, the wrong Walworth that called him. There had been in her voice a tension he was unable to define. Was it merely that she was about to become troublesome? Was she the type? he had no really clear impression of her. He passed a few moments trying to visualize her, and found, as he expected, that no distinct image responded. All the meetings with her had been in the dimly-lighted hall; also, his Linda-trouble, for the time being, rendered him more or less oblivious to all women. He did retain an impression of an extremely youthful creature, of a girl about eighteen at most. And now it seemed that her crush was about to move into its nuisance phase; in addition to all his current problems, would he have to deal with that too?

As he mechanically took his hat and topcoat and left the office, he was sure of one thing; that if Miss Ann Walworth descended on him during office-hours, he would have a nurse present during every moment of the interview.

CHAPTER 9

Connie, sitting in the Mount Peace Chapel, slewed her eyes sideways for the dozenth time at Myra, sitting decorously beside her. She saw the still-pretty profile, slightly lifted toward the minister, the smart black hat and suit, and just the edge, fresh and crisp, of the white frill on her blouse. Myra's face was clear, her manner untroubled; yesterday's agitation had been wiped away as though it had never been. Her relief at getting hold of Archie's diaries (it was clear to Connie) had not only completely restored her equanimity, but had buttressed her self-approval with a touch of swagger, of cockiness. Connie smiled to herself, imperceptibly.

The Office for the Dead proceeded movingly, according to its appointed forms, but from the first words she had been deaf, immersed completely in debating her policy with regard to Myra. Should she come down on her at once with a demand for money? This was the first question. But again, had she really enough on Myra to bring it off successfully? This was the second question, even more crucial than the first. Since yesterday Connie had balanced one against the other, with no result but the fatigue of indecision.

The entry in Archie's journal was startling, no doubt; it strongly suggested dirty work in connection with a family death. But it was fatally lacking in confirmatory detail, offering not the slightest hint as to the when, or, most important — the *how* of the crime. Suppose — in spite of her misgivings as to these weak links — suppose she made her blackmail attempt; suppose Myra dared her to prove anything; what, actually, could she prove? The bare possibility of her bluff being called had kept her in a torment of vacillation for twenty-four hours, paralyzing her will to act. It was maddening, tantalizing, she reflected; having something on Myra, but not really enough. Should she try it anyhow? or should she wait, in hopes of unearthing more concrete proof? and what proof could she hope to unearth, at this late day? So it all circled back to the one question: tackle Myra at once? yes or no?

She sat pursuing the question round and round in her mind, thinking, debating . . . and suddenly, there in the chapel with the small group – not a dozen – collected in the forward pews, the answer burst upon her, lighting up her mental landscape as with the naked glare of a starshell.

Myra had no idea at all of the diary's contents.

This, Connie saw belatedly, was her trump card; the impregnable strength of her position. The empty places in Archie's recital, the dismaying gaps, were her secret alone; for all Myra knew, she might have in her hands the fullest most circumstantial description of the crime, instead of what she actually possessed – a series of oblique allusions, half-stated – or implied rather than stated. Yes – she would put her cards on the table at once; she would make her demand. Then she would guide herself according to the reactions of her mother-in-law. She *might* have to bluff somewhat, in view of Myra's fiendish talent for smelling out the weak place, but she fervently hoped not. A final wave of faintheartedness swept over her, to be summarily dismissed. She must risk the attempt, and at once; later might be too late. Also there was the value – not to be ignored – of shock-tactics.

Having made the port of final decision, Connie relaxed in the pew, with an unconscious sigh, and woke once more to the proceedings in the chapel. The minister's voice had ceased, the organ had begun playing. Upon the air mounted *Jesu, Joy of Man's Desiring*, its ascending triplet figuration renewing itself constantly from some inner source of power, building higher and higher like a sky-aspiring steeple, an architecture of longing; from time to time the chorale struck in with its brief, almost curt, affirmation of faith. Archie's sister and niece-by-marriage, on less than nodding terms with Bach, were unaware that Mr. Combs had borne in mind his client's special love for this music, and had requested it.

Connie noted briefly that the coffin was surprisingly small as, on its carrier, it glided past her toward the chapel door in rubber-tired silence, almost stealth. When it disappeared, the congregation rose.

"The crematory's only a few blocks away," whispered Myra. "So convenient."

"Well, I'll be seeing you," said Myra, her black-gloved fingers on the handle of her car door. She flicked a glance at Connie's convertible, parked behind her. "I was willing to pick you up," she complained. "I don't think you should have driven that thing to a funeral — awfully unsuitable."

"I'm going on somewhere from here,"

Connie explained. Myra shrugged, opening the door of her sleek black car, discreetly chromium-banded.

"Well —" she turned on Connie the slightest edge of a smile. "If I were you, darling, I'd start looking around for that job." She got into the car and slammed the door, then waved a small hand airily through the window.

Before and behind them the five or six cars of the cortège were starting up and driving away with that briskness and relief peculiar to after funerals. Myra's car nosed out from the curb, and in a moment was running smoothly and powerfully down the street; at a distance of half-a-block, Connie's car followed her.

Myra's sedan was already put away, and its owner crossing toward the house, when Connie's car drew up on the wide asphalt turn-around before the garage. Myra stopped dead on seeing her.

"Why, whatever —?" she demanded, as Connie got out. "What in the world?"

"I remembered something I wanted to ask you," Connie returned easily.

"But to follow me all the way here — I never heard of such a thing! Why didn't you honk? I know your horn — I'd have stopped."

"I had to see you here," said Connie. They were now walking side by side along the driveway, toward the front of the house.

"Couldn't you have phoned?" Myra demanded, the first hint of petulance in her voice.

"Not so very well," said Connie.

Myra stopped dead again. "Look, darling," she said. "To tell the truth, I was planning to lie down – all this has tired me out more than I thought. What do you want? is it money again?"

"Not exactly."

"Not exactly!" Myra's echo combined irony and indignation. "Now see here, Connie," she went on, with extreme incisiveness. "Just get rid of this idea of yours that I owe you anything. I've let you get away with it 'til now, and you know for whose sake – not for yours. But it's *enough*, as of this minute – you've done it one time too many. You have no claim on me, do you understand? Once and for all, you've no claim on me whatever. You ought to be ashamed, a strong young woman," she wound up on a high note of rebuke, "hounding a sick old one for money." Though totally repudiating the thought of age in connection with herself, Myra was not above claiming it whenever it might give her an advantage. "So that's all I have to say to you – you needn't come into the house."

"All the same, I really have to," Connie persisted smoothly. It was then — at the front door — that Myra turned full around and surveyed Connie's blandness and faint smile with the first flicker of perplexity — and of something else, as yet imperceptible. Then she unlocked the door, pushed it open brusquely and went through, Connie on her heels. In the hall Myra turned and faced her daughter-in-law.

"Make it short," she commanded. "I want to lie down."

"Let's go upstairs," Connie suggested.

Myra's eyes began shooting sparks. "Now I don't want to get mean," she articulated, like splintered glass. "But you'll make me, in a minute. Say what you have to say here, or don't say it at all."

"Upstairs," Connie murmured. "We'd better, we'd really better." She was immovably, ominously pleasant; Myra stared at her — and once again, behind her eyes, flickered that something of a few seconds past, evident now and definable; the beginnings of apprehension. Myra was totally a creature of instinct, and even then, perhaps, had some obscure foreknowledge of what was coming. After a moment she compressed her lips, walked past Connie and upstairs; Connie followed her.

Once in the bedroom, Connie closed the door, sat down uninvited, and watched Myra benignly as she jerked off the little black hat, threw it onto the chaise longue, and followed it with the jacket of her suit. Then she sat down squarely on the slipper chair, riveted her eyes on Connie, and waited.

"I understand," Connie began, agreeably, "that you went to the san yesterday and took Archie's diaries."

Myra was silent a moment; to her inimical glance was added cool inquiry — also a degree, unmistakable, of wariness.

"Well, why not?" she queried, but choosing her words with obvious care. "After all, diaries — they're personal — they're family papers. I didn't see why those snoopy nurses should read them so I took them. That's all there was to it."

"What did you do with them?"

"I burned them," Myra shrugged. "I burned them without even looking at them. Archie and his diaries! he always kept one, just like an old maid. After a person's gone you can't keep that kind of litter around — it's no good to anyone any more. And what of it?" she demanded. A shade of relief was beginning to pervade her, but that reliable instinct of hers kept her from relaxing prematurely. "What business is it of yours?"

"None," Connie assured her cheerfully.

"Well then? —"

"But maybe —" Connie paused a moment, deliberately; her voice fell a little lower. Myra heard, felt it; she seemed to cringe, a plump hen feeling the hawk's shadow. "— maybe," Connie went on, "you didn't notice something. The diaries in the drawer were old diaries. I guess you didn't check the dates, or else you'd have seen —" she smiled right into Myra's eyes "— you'd have seen the latest one was missing — the one for this year. He didn't keep that one in the drawer at all. It stood on top of his desk — the current diary."

A silence fell in the room; neither woman moved.

"I have it," Connie said softly.

The silence fell again — a deeper silence. Myra still stared, her movelessness taking on a stony quality; then it happened, as Connie had known it would happen. She watched her mother-in-law's face become old, suffused with the dull, ugly flush; the eyes turn watery, the shoulders sag. Composedly she got up, opened Myra's bag and placed it close to her. Seeing her unable to stir, Connie found the bottle, placed the glass rod between her lips. Then, with detachment, she waited for signs of recovery; these seemed a little longer in

110

coming than on the previous day. Still, Myra was coming around; her eyes, emptied of everything but pain, regained reason and focus, and fixed themselves on her daughter-in-law with an expression so remarkable as to jolt, for the moment, even Connie. Then, as the older woman still sat motionless and silent, "The very first time I mentioned the diaries, you threw one of these attacks," she remarked conversationally. "I didn't connect the two things right away — how could I? I hadn't looked at the current diary — yet." She paused a moment before stepping, with outer confidence but inner misgiving, onto the thinnest ice of all. "But I certainly don't wonder at your being knocked out. I'd be knocked out myself — with what Archie's put down in that little green book of his."

She waited, hardly breathing; this was the crucial moment. If Myra should challenge her, say lightly, "I don't believe you have anything really; do anything you like with it and see how far you get —" then Connie's edifice, of too much conjecture and too little fact, would be shown up for what it was beneath that mocking stare. But she heard nothing but the silence, stretching out moment after moment; her heart began pounding victoriously. Myra was not going to challenge anything; it was obvious that her inner knowledge of guilt, combined with the menace of Connie's weapon – the diary – shook her to the foundations. After an interval, moving her eyes from Connie's face and fixing them on one end of the dressing-table, she moistened her lips and asked, almost inaudibly, "What do you want?"

Connie was more than ready to answer, but Myra was continuing, still in that breathless ghost of a voice, "A thousand – I could let you have a thousand. In six months, another thousand. Every six months, the same."

"Thanks," Connie murmured. "I'll take – for a starter – ten thousand."

"Ten thousand!" It shrilled out of Myra with sudden, incredible force, considering her aura of collapse. "Why – why – what do you – where do you think I'd get ten thousand?" Her voice failed momentarily, recovered. "Do you think I keep that much – lying around – in cash?"

"Oh no," said Connie, amiably. "But you have stocks or bonds or whatever, you can sell a few – turn them into cash. Nothing to it."

"That's my – my capital," gasped Myra, like a spent swimmer threshing in the water.

"Not much of your capital," Connie responded soothingly. "And how much of your income? only three hundred a year or so –

you'll never miss it. I'm sure," she went on nonchalantly, "you could get it by tomorrow, or day after tomorrow at the latest." She added, as an afterthought, "In tens, twenties and fifties, please."

Myra sat leadenly; Connie allowed the silence to spin itself out a while longer, then correctly judged that little was to be expected from her mother-in-law in the way of conversation, and rose easily, as from an afternoon call. "I'll be around – let's see – day-after-tomorrow, shall I?"

"Don't you – don't you –" Myra's voice was a strangled whisper, and she fought hard to get even that out. "– don't you ever – do this again, ever again – don't you *dare.*"

"Day-after-tomorrow," Connie repeated gently, and walked out of the room, leaving Myra staring after her.

Ann, her heart in her mouth, tiptoed downstairs at the utmost rate of speed compatible with perfect silence. Almost as soon as the bedroom door had closed behind the two, she had been pressed against it, her ear glued to the panel, while her eyes ceaselessly, nervously canvassed avenues of escape, in case either of them came out suddenly. The nearest door was across the hall; could she disappear through it quickly enough? or get down the stairs in time? . . .

Now – though her vigil had lasted only a few minutes – some warning instinct, rather than anything she had heard, drove her headlong back to her own room. To run the risk of being caught eavesdropping – how shabby; but to this resort her sense of extreme urgency had compelled her, fortified by Myra's voice in the hall, directly they had returned from the funeral. She had sounded so curiously hostile – *beleaguered;* and there, mixed up in it again, was Connie . . . willy-nilly, she had to take the chance.

But fortune was with her to the degree that she got safely into her room – and heard overhead, almost instantly, the sound of the opening door. Standing motionless, her own door almost closed but not quite, she heard Connie come down with her usual light step, except that her heels seemed to bite into the bare polished wood with an unaccustomed definiteness. Then the hall door opened, banged back – without latching, she could tell by the sound; an inveterate habit of Connie's, one of those minute actions that seem to limn, as with a sudden glare, a rooted, crass inconsiderateness.

There followed the sound of her car driving

away, then a long interval of quiet. Ann sat unmoving, a silent vessel full to the brim of cold dread and conjecture, formless imaginings and alarm. The interview in Myra's room, in spite of her concentrated eavesdropping, had told her little; it had been — for the most part — conducted in so low a key that she had retrieved only disconnected words. Connie had seemed to be doing most of the talking, amiably enough. Both of them, for that matter, had sounded merely conversational; at this stage she had heard the word *diary* several times. Suddenly there had followed what struck Ann with foreboding. A silence; she could not get that heavy, ugly silence out of her ears. Then — shockingly, and like the other day — had come that wild scream from Myra. Only this time she had heard the words; *ten thousand!* Then more words, inaudible, in a gasping, failing voice, and then — worst of all — that horrid, hoarse whispering, nightmarish. It was at this point that she had taken to flight — just in time; if anything more had passed upstairs, she had missed it.

Carefully she began taking stock of the situation, which seemed to divide itself into two parts. One, the mysterious goings-on between Myra and Connie; two, the effect of these encounters on Myra. About the first she felt hopeless; she could evolve no plan of action when perfectly ignorant of what she was up against. But the second – for dealing with that, she was on firmer ground. Connie had seen Myra twice, each time with the worst effect on Myra. Obviously, therefore, she must be prevented from seeing Myra again; that much was clear as crystal.

Once more she issued from her room, and moved softly toward the pantry door. Before going through, however, she tilted her head upward and stood listening. In the unbroken silence – utterly uncharacteristic of Myra – there seemed something doomed, stricken; the sense of mystery and dread settled on her again, and the cold lump inside her became heavier.

Retreating noiselessly through the pantry door, she lifted the extension phone, gave a number. At least her phone call of the other day (what a fool she must have sounded to him, blurting and being tongue-tied by turns) had put her in possession of his office-hours. When a woman's voice replied, she said resolutely, "I'd like to make an appointment with Dr. Markham today, please, at five-thirty or after. Not today? But I must, it's urgent. No, tomorrow won't do. He can squeeze me in somehow," she calmly overrode the protesting

116

nurse. "I'll be there at five-thirty this evening."

Ushered in by Miss Rogers, she entered his office and instantly divined the mood behind his impersonal greeting; the nurse had reported her insistence, and he objected to her crashing his office hours.

"He's annoyed," she thought. "Let him." Her fixity of purpose fortified her, surmounting even the shortness of breath and weakening of knees that his presence always evoked.

"Sit down, Miss Walworth," he said in a cool, disinterested voice; and Ann sat. "Now," he continued, with a professional inflection that was also subtly reproving, "what seems to be the trouble?"

Ann, instead of replying, swivelled her head toward a point behind, and a few feet distant from her — where, in obedience to her employer's instructions, the nurse stood inconspicuously beside the door. When she turned to face him again, a sudden color flushed her cheeks, and her eyes flashed squarely into his; the doctor experienced a sudden and unexpected discomfort.

"I'd like to talk to you privately, doctor," said Ann. The steel in her voice surprised her no less than him. *What must he think of me,* she demanded of herself inwardly, hot with shame all over her body. *Is he afraid I'll jump him, or what?* The cautery of resentment sealed off, for the moment, even the pain of unwanted love; she turned hard, composed and cold as ice, and for this she was inexpressibly grateful. "Privately – *if* you don't mind," she added, hearing the words emerge crisp and definite; her voice was not giving her away in the least.

"I – ah –" Ralph began in what was nearly a stammer, and a sharp satisfaction lifted her inwardly; at least she had given him a moment of embarrassment. *Serve you right,* she thought.

"I usually have Miss Rogers present," Ralph lied, with insufficient prevision, "when I see patients."

"Always?" Her lifted eyebrows, all but mocking him, made short work of his assertion. "I have to speak to you privately," she iterated, and was rewarded by seeing him raise his eyes and make an imperceptible signal to the woman standing behind her. The door opened and closed softly; she sat straight and scornful, pointedly oblivious of the sound.

"I hate you," she informed him silently, with longing, "Of all the luck – to be in love with you."

"She's not quite the infant I took her for," reflected Ralph. "But very, very young – hasn't jelled yet." Wryly aware that she had made him feel not only like a fool, but an apologetic fool, he was brusque as he said, "Yes, Miss Walworth — what can I do for you?"

Ann took a long breath, and nerved herself to expose her improbable — and piecemeal — story to the dispassionate regard opposite her; it even flashed through her mind that he might suspect her of inventing it, as a means of attracting his attention. But she had asked for this interview; she must plow ahead, for better or worse.

"I — I — that is, my sister-in-law, Mrs. Walworth —" there she was, floundering as she had feared she would do. Pulling up quickly, she took a firm grip of herself and tried again. "Mrs. Walworth is doing something to my mother that — that will certainly injure her health, if she isn't stopped."

The doctor waited, without comment.

"Twice now Connie's seen her," Ann went on, "and each time, there's been a scene." She stopped short, looked at him hopefully.

"A scene," he repeated. "You mean raised voices?"

"Not specially," she returned. "But each time, my mother screamed, once — she actually *screamed.*"

"As with pain?" he inquired, with raised

brows. "Or temper?"

They exchanged the faintest of smiles at this broad diagnosis, but she sobered at once and answered, "Not with pain — and I wouldn't say with temper, exactly. It was more like —" she was listening intently to the remembered sound. "— like rage, or . . ." she groped "— there was a *wild* sound to it. Desperate," she said suddenly. That was it, of course. "Desperate," she repeated.

"Have you any idea of the nature of these interviews? what the trouble was?"

"I haven't — but not for want of trying." Her look — of mingled awkwardness and defiance — made her seem younger than ever. "I listened at the door the second time — I thought I might have to interfere. But I couldn't hear anything much — not enough to go on, at any rate."

He was silent a moment, then queried, "What do you want me to do?" Her haughty astonishment tickled him unexpectedly, as she replied, "I want you to keep Mrs. Walworth from seeing my mother."

"But my dear young lady —" her heart seized hungrily on this attenuated endearment "— my dear young lady, I'm only a doctor, not an arbitrator. I can't interfere between your mother and her daughter-in-law," he explained

— then, seeing her about to interrupt angrily, "Your mother herself might be the first to resent it."

This stopped her, he was glad to see; but not for long. Her shoulders squared themselves anew, her remorseless eyes took a fresh grip of him, and he wilted inwardly.

"My mother's your patient," she threw at him. "Can't you protect your patient? I'm telling you, after those two dust-ups with Connie, she looked like death. You yourself —" she impaled him with a hortatory hazel glance "— you said that being upset or worried was the worst possible thing for her."

"I'll tell you what," bargained Ralph, feeling cornered. Pertinacious was not the word for it; the child would hang on until she got what she wanted. "Persuade your mother to call me in on this. If *she* complains to me, I can forbid Mrs. Walworth to see her. But I can only do it on your mother's complaint, not on yours." But she was shaking her head vigorously before he finished.

"Mamma mustn't know I came to see you," she said with urgency. "If she had the least idea I'd been talking about her affairs and interfering like this —!"

"Well then — couldn't you talk to your sister-in-law? couldn't you talk to Mrs. Walworth?"

At this query — a reasonable one, it seemed to him — a startling expression flashed over her face, and was gone in an instant. Very good features she had, and exceptionally beautiful skin, he noted for the first time; but then his longest meeting with her had been for a few seconds, in the dusty entrance-hall. All this, however, interested him less than the unguarded look that had escaped her for that fraction of a second. If he knew repugnance and revulsion — to an extraordinary degree — he had just seen them; if he knew fear, he had seen that too.

"No," she answered briefly, averting her eyes. "I couldn't possibly talk to Mrs. Walworth." She made no attempt to qualify her flat refusal; he thought sardonically, after his first moment of surprise, *Jealousy?*

Meanwhile she had risen to her feet.

"Make some excuse to see Mamma," she petitioned. "Something's wrong, awfully wrong — you'll see it as soon as you look at her. Please get to see her somehow, will you? *Will* you?"

"I'll try," he found himself promising, surprised that he had capitulated to the iron purpose in that youthful frame.

"Thank you," she almost whispered, for a blind, mendicant longing possessed her suddenly, a longing to hold her arms out to him ... hastily she lowered her eyes to the glove she was putting on the wrong hand, then, unexpectedly, smiled at him, a brief impish smile. "Better call in Miss Rogers, hadn't you?" she inquired solicitously, "so she can see you're all right?"

While he experienced an unwonted lack of anything to say, she walked out of the office.

For a few seconds, staring thoughtfully before him, Ralph delayed buzzing Miss Rogers and telling her she could go. A queer story, this, about Connie's dire effect on her mother-in-law. The daughter was exaggerating, no doubt. Still, the girl's personality hardly suggested a liar, a misrepresenter ... and then her peculiar reaction to her sister-in-law's name ... still, every family had its odd situations and tensions, without doubt.

Now he found that the mention of Connie's name had brought her image before him again, vividly. That slender voluptuousness, that unspoken challenge ... it dawned on him suddenly that he might have gotten her phone-number from Ann, with this Myra situation as a pretext; he had had the perfect opportunity and muffed it.

He cursed his stupidity briefly and sincerely. At the same moment, however, there was slowly, unwillingly forming in him the conviction that it was important — even imperative — to create an occasion for seeing Myra Walworth as soon as possible.

CHAPTER 10

Mr. Landis, the nice young teller at the bank, was host to a number of perplexities, all of them on Mrs. Walworth's account. In the first place, he had happened that morning to be in the office of Mr. Hulse, the bank-manager, when she had phoned with instructions to convert certain of her holdings in sufficient amount to raise ten thousand dollars. She wished this done as soon as possible, she added, and would call for it next day or the day after.

Both men had exchanged expressions of mild surprise; Mrs. Walworth had banked there for years, and the pattern of her financial habits was as familiar and predictable to Mr. Hulse as to Mr. Landis, whose window she favored. Her checking-account never rose above, nor fell below, a certain level; against it, month after month, she made the same withdrawals. And now, suddenly, and on a moment's notice — this need for ten thousand dollars?

"She must be going to Europe," conjectured Mr. Hulse.

"Probably," concurred Mr. Landis. "Next thing, traveller's checks."

"I wouldn't wonder," said Mr. Hulse, and busied himself according to Mrs. Walworth's directions. This was simple; everything listed in her name was highly negotiable — a lovely list of stuff, a small estate in beautiful shape, Mr. Hulse reflected; he considered Mrs. Walworth an extremely shrewd woman.

On the forenoon of the next day, however, he received another phone-call, as a result of which he left his office, frowning with exasperation, and sought Mr. Landis.

"Mrs. Walworth wants that ten thousand in cash," he said, adding with sarcasm, "She forgot to tell me yesterday."

"Ten thousand in cash!" echoed Mr. Landis.

"Ten, twenties and fifties, and only this minute gave me the glad tidings," said Mr. Hulse. "Make it up, will you?"

As a result of this exchange, and in the intervals of waiting on other depositors, Mr. Landis was still counting industriously at two-thirty-five, at which hour Mrs. Walworth herself appeared, taking up her stand at his window, where no one else happened to be at the moment.

Mr. Landis glanced up from his occupation to say good-morning – and received a shock. He had always considered Mrs. Walworth an extremely attractive woman, in his innocence under-estimating her age by a good many years, and his formula in regard to her was, "I'll bet she was a knockout, in her day." Invariably he completed the formula by assuring himself, "And I'll bet she hasn't missed anything, either." He liked her smart clothes and gay manner, her expensive perfume and knowing blue eyes, he enjoyed the pleasantries – the "joshing" – that enlivened any encounter between them.

But with the woman on whom Mr. Landis's eyes had just fallen, there would be no joshing. Puffed and wattled cheeks, drooping lips tightly compressed, dull, red-lidded eyes fixed on distance; no greeting even, no least acknowledgement. This old woman – twenty years older at least than *his* Mrs. Walworth – had surrounded herself with a forbidding aura of coldness and remoteness, as foreign to him as her incredibly altered appearance.

The riot of conjectures that surged through Mr. Landis's mind failed, however, to interrupt the rhythm of his counting. It was a small bank with only three cashiers, and people were entering now in droves, the usual last-minute rush; Mr. Landis was aware of the line piling up behind Mrs. Walworth, and it made him nervous. And still the notes spun from his flying fingers, still the neat piles mounted, stacked crosswise by hundreds, then by thousands, and after that a second counting. At this point Mr. Landis began to dislike Mrs. Walworth, for the first time in their acquaintance. To pull a thing like this half-an-hour before closing time! These old country-club biddies were all alike; they thought the village people existed solely for their convenience. Mentally he applied to Mrs. Walworth a term that would have horrified his mother, who was a great power in the Baptist Ladies' Aid, and who had brought him up to think respectfully of women.

The bell of St. Martin's, nearby, started bonging; on the final vibrations of the three massive strokes, the notes were counted, recounted, and assembled into a compact mass the size of a small brick.

"Would you like these in envelopes —" Mr. Landis began.

"Just give it here," Mrs. Walworth interrupted him in a cold, distant voice. Without a word of thanks she took the packet, crammed it down into her big bag, turned abruptly, and walked out of the door, where Laura Conover had stood since the stroke of three, waiting to shut up shop.

"Don't mention it, Mrs. Walworth," Mr. Landis said to himself caustically. "A pleasure, Mrs. Walworth." Then suddenly there struck him another reason for her wanting so large a sum of money; a reason which had not before occurred to him.

"Gosh," he thought with compunction, "an operation. That's it — a serious operation." (*But why in cash? and in just those denominations?* his unconscious demanded.) Still — "I bet that's it," he ruminated. The more he thought the more reasonable it sounded, and as a sequel to his meditations he liked Mrs. Walworth again, was worried about her, and apologized to her mentally. Mr. Landis might look rather prissy with his slicked-down black hair, sallow face and long thin nose, but all the same he was as kind a young man as one would wish to meet.

CHAPTER 11

Through the November day, unseasonable in its mildness, Connie walked lazily up to Lydia's house. The brilliant red berries of the barberry hedge denied the almost-hot sunshine; the faint smoke of burning leaves lay incongruous on the balmy windless air. The peace of her surroundings, blending pleasantly with her newfound peace of mind, combined to produce in her a mood soporific, almost benign. What a contrast, between her recent torment, the penny-worries, the penny-pinching, and this relaxed, drowsy well-being! And what had effected the transformation? just one thing, one little simple thing, reflected Connie, and lovingly patted the pocket of her green suit − already she thought of it as her *old* suit − where reposed five twenty-dollar bills.

"There's nothing like you, sweeties," she crooned half-aloud. "Nothing like you in all the world."

The big shambles of a living-room was

deserted, except for five or six ruffled, tiny fox-faces, whose bright beady stare conveyed pre-ternatural alertness and — it seemed — no very complimentary opinion; one or two of them let loose a couple of yaps, piercing but perfunctory, for of course they knew her perfectly well. A hail up the stairs, then through the kitchen door, produced no response in the big barn of a place, so she went outdoors again and around to the back, where stood Lydia's workroom-office, a converted garage; her disreputable car stood outside the year around, taking its chances with all weathers.

The door was closed but unlocked, and Connie stepped into a whitewashed room about twenty by sixteen. Here Lydia made out bills, prepared dogfood, clipped and bathed clients, and administered simple treatments and remedies. The mare'snest look of the room dissimulated a certain rough system; also, where cleanliness was required, it was absolute — as evidenced by the scrubbed porcelain kitchen table and the brand-new sterilizer that stood against the wall, puffing and steaming with an air of pent-up purpose.

"Close the door!" Lydia bawled at once. She was lifting down from the table a four-months-old boarder to whom she had just administered its second puppy-distemper shot; the boarder began running about the room with an air of release, of renewed trust in mankind, and of willingness to overlook the late unpleasant incident.

"He's not bad," ruminated Lydia, following the puppy with her eyes. "A bit shallow in the jaw, maybe – too soon to tell." She was always conducting soliloquies with herself about animals, regardless of her company. "Not one of mine, of course." She turned a jaundiced eye on Connie. "What's on your mind, whiskey-panhandler?"

"Here's the balance of what I owe you," said Connie airily, taking from her pocket the small roll of bills.

"Not on the table!" shrieked Lydia, snatching the money just in the nick of time. "I just swabbed it down with alcohol." Her eyes settled on the bills, widened. "The whole thing? what's happened to you, for God's sake? hit the jackpot?"

"Not exactly," murmured Connie. *Jackpot*, she thought to herself, with an inward grin; *that's it, a female jackpot, and I certainly hit it.*

"Well, is this a Godsend! and can I use it!" Lydia blew out her breath noisily, with large and undisguised relief. "Now I can hold out 'til the weekend. I've a woman coming from New York Saturday or Sunday, it's almost a sure bet that she'll take those two babies of Amorette's at three hundred and fifty per. If she doesn't, I'd better find some nice deep water somewhere and make a hole in it."

She continued to talk, but Connie was no longer listening; her eyes had settled on the table, where lay the hypodermic Lydia had just been using — a small one, the regulation ten cc. At sight of it, her casual glance had become riveted; something flicked at her memory, on its outermost boundaries, and was gone. It reminded her of something, or rather it ought to remind her of something, if only she could remember what; with a sudden, prickling urgency she felt it important, tremendously important, that she should remember ... mechanically, almost mindlessly, she reached toward it; Lydia instantly slapped her hand away.

"Don't touch it!" she snapped. "Those things cost like all get out — fiddle around with it and drop it or something, and bang, four dollars shot to hell. Get away from the table, anyway," she commanded. "It's sterile — I told you."

"All right," shrugged Connie. "I just wanted to pay up." She turned toward the door, then halted. "By the way, Lyd — I might be moving before long."

"Moving!" ejaculated Lydia. Her eyes

widened again. "Sweet Jesus, you *are* in the money, aren't you? Did you murder a relative? And where're you moving? when?"

"Oh, it's not immediate," Connie returned hastily. "When I go, *if* I go, I'll give you plenty of notice."

"Do, for God's sake," said Lydia. "It's tough renting a place in Winter, especially a beat-up shack in the sticks. Gatehouse, they call it!" she snorted. "Outhouse would be more like it." As she spoke she was disassembling the hypodermic, dropping its parts into the sterilizer — and again Connie's eyes followed the glass-and-steel glitter with that half-sense of something forgotten, something vital, that she must at all costs recapture.

Moreover, once again in her living-room, her meditations had lost their fine sunny flavor; a familiar haze of anxiety began thickening on their outer edges, gradually encircling her, moving in upon her. In this gloomier mood she started to evaluate, more realistically, her situation — that same situation which only a few minutes ago had seemed so rosy.

What was ten thousand dollars? a convenient sum certainly, an interlude of relief, in her case a miraculous rescue, no less. *But* — and it was a large but — it bore no relation whatever to the question of permanent, or nearly permanent, security. With care she could live on it sixteen or eighteen months — with a constant sense of her resources draining away beneath her — then find herself back precisely where she had started. No, what she needed was fifty or a hundred thousand, not ten; which brought up, like the vision of a volcanic eruption or similar lurid convulsion of nature, the question of Myra's probable behavior if faced with the larger demand. True, she had been unresisting the first time, almost passive, for her — but Connie was shrewd enough to divine this as partly the result of shock; the sudden disclosure of her secret, the unexpectedness of the attack, had thrown her off balance. But given time to recover her footing, and faced with the loss of a quarter or a half of her resources . . . that was something else again, Connie acknowledged; inevitably Myra would rouse herself, she would really begin to fight. Picturing the quality of the battle that her mother-in-law could still put up if pressed, she shrank a little, involuntarily.

Suppose she made her demand; suppose Myra, in desperation, defied her, refused, challenged her to do her worst; what next? She would be left standing there, impotent, shown up as a maker of empty threats. If Archie, damn him, had only given her a *little* more to go on than that dream of his . . . again something touched Connie's memory, having to do with dreams, it seemed — then flickered away, leaving her with a vague, irritated feeling that it was important, if only she could have gotten hold of it.

In the end she was left with nothing but a sour conviction that her weapons were too flimsy to risk in a showdown, and that an unsuccessful attempt was at all costs to be avoided — for it would expose her to a too-percipient Myra as having negotiated her previous coup by means of bluff. Let it once dawn on Myra that she had been bluffed out of ten thousand dollars . . . at the thought, Connie quailed again. No, a second demand was out of the question, for the present; she needed much more information, of a nature conclusive enough to brace and revivify her sinews of extortion.

Connie laughed aloud, a brief, bitter laugh. By what miracle was she to exhume the dope on a murder twelve years old, not even suspected as murder at the time of its accomplishment?

She averted her thoughts despairingly from the hopelessness of the project; lifelessly, without interest, she picked up the local newspaper, a tri-weekly. Her eyes wandered over it indifferently, half-unseeing; her thoughts were far removed from neighborhood chronicles.

Two minutes later she sat up straight all at once, and reread an item under *Personals:* she had read it once before without realizing its import.

Mr. Theodore Gedney has returned from a year's stay in Europe, and is located temporarily at the Vale Park Country Club, prior to moving to New York. Mr. Gedney entertained at dinner last Tuesday for his sister and niece, Mrs. Myra Walworth and Miss Ann Walworth, of Old Mill Drive, Three Elms Twp.

So fat Theo was back from Europe, once more making complete in America the tale of all four Gedney inheritors, dead and alive.

For some minutes Connie sat motionless, chewing over this most recent development. Her degree of acquaintance with Theo, less than intimate, was sufficient for phoning him under some pretext or other.

. . . we went downstairs and waited for the others. . . .

It was still her theory that Theo had been one of *the others*, and here, if at all, was her chance at attempting to verify it. A little nudging of the conversation into the right channels, and he might let something slip . . . had he been an active part of the murder plan? or was he, perhaps, quite ignorant of it, since he had not been present? On the other hand, might this absence of his have been deliberate, prearranged? had it served some purpose in the total design?

Well, to sit here beating her brains out with guesswork — thanks to Archie's reprehensible failure to be specific — would certainly get her no further forward. She must speak to Theo, *see* him, appraise his expressions, the changes in his voice, measure delicately these minims, these almost-shadows. . . . She looked up the club number, reached quickly for the phone — then checked, considering her line of approach. A loan — that would sound plausible; she would give him a hard-luck story, extort a personal interview by hook or by crook. Not that she expected from him a decisive clue — that would be fantastic; but he might unwittingly provide her with a lead, some kind, any kind, so long as it was new; she had gone as far as she could on what she had, and now stood before a blank wall, desperate. If Theo had actually participated in murder, he was a commodity rapidly becoming rarer; of the original four, one had been cancelled out by death, and another by senility. Yes, she must nail him before his excess fat rolled him over with a fatal stroke, or something ... lifting the receiver, she gave the number of the Vale Park Country Club.

CHAPTER 12

"Tormenting me, all of you!" Myra raged. "All of you!" She burst into strangling sobs.

Ann, painfully moved but calm, stood unanswering beneath the tirade, so unlike, so utterly unlike, Myra; having brought it on by her persuasion that Myra would see the doctor. Her mother's temper was set on a hairspring nowadays, and any trifle was likely to touch it off. And along with this emotional deterioration went a corresponding physical one; in the last couple of weeks she had even stopped making up, except for lipstick carelessly applied, and her skin looked white and flaccid, suddenly webbed with hundreds of tiny lines.

And it hurt to see this, Ann discovered with surprise; it hurt excessively. No matter that she had been aware, for years, of the lack of any real sympathy between them; it was unbearable to see her mother so crippled in spirit as to relinquish, with such ruinous completeness, her vigilantly-preserved youth, by far her chief preoccupation and most precious possession. The sight stirred up in Ann not only a most unsettling pain of compassion, but something else; a renewed affection which, from being perfunctory for many years, suddenly flared into protectiveness.

I must do something, Ann thought, waiting for Myra's sobs to subside; *I can't let her be battered around like this. I must find out what's going on here, and do something.*

Myra suddenly turned on her; her smeared red mouth took on an ugly shape, as in the old masks of Tragedy.

"Don't stand there looking at me!" she shrieked, and with a heart-breaking gesture tried to cover her hair with her hands, thereby drawing Ann's attention to something she had never seen before. "Get out! get out!"

Ann escaped into the hall, where she stood in almost-awed consideration of the new phenomenon – the chalkline around Myra's contorted face, where the neglected red curls had grown white, an even quarter-of-an-inch all around. Myra letting herself go white; the upheaval of planets was less staggering to an astronomer than this spectacle to Ann. Of what inner collapse was this the evidence? of what total self-abandonment to despair?

If Connie should materialize before her at

this moment, she felt, it would be a pleasure to put her hands around her neck, and squeeze hard.

While the maid went upstairs to announce him to Mrs. Walworth, Dr. Markham waited in the hall in the irritable awareness that he was paying an unsolicited call upon a patient, for the first time in his life. His resentment centered chiefly upon Ann, as being responsible, and his state of mind hardly improved when he happened to glance upstairs. Myra was standing there, silently regarding him over the bannister; for how long, he had no idea.

"Good day, Mrs. Walworth," he greeted her, with false heartiness. "I was passing by, and thought I'd ask you for a cup of coffee." It was not very good, but it was the best he could think of. "I could have it alone somewhere, but why have it alone when I could have it with you?" This note of semi-flirtatious badinage was, he knew, the one to which she most readily responded. Only, this time, she responded not at all; he was surprised at her blank stillness, uncharacteristic. Also, even in the dimness of the hall and at a number of yards distant from her, he was aware of something curious about her appearance, something very much out-of-the-way. Suddenly and urgently he wanted to see her in a good light, and at close quarters.

"What about that cup of coffee?" he went on. "Or are you busy?"

"Come up," said Myra briefly; then to the maid, just coming out of her room, "Bring Dr. Markham a pot of coffee, will you, Bessie — and some cookies or something if we have any."

"Cookies too!" the doctor congratulated himself, as he came up. "I knew I'd had myself a good idea."

Myra preceded him into her room and stood motionless, her back to him, until Bessie had gotten downstairs and along the hall into the kitchen.

Then she turned and faced him.

The doctor experienced a moment of unbelief, of consternation — and of inward, unconscious apology to Ann. The Myra he had last seen, barely a month ago, had been trim, jaunty, successful in holding off ten or more years of her age; the woman before him was flabby, raddled, carelessly dressed and made up, undisguisedly old. And there were other, much more disturbing aspects of her appearance. Her heart-condition had been of the slightest — incipient almost — promising, in a woman who took such devoted care of herself, to be almost static for many years; now, his eye took in several well-defined symptoms of a much more ominous nature. There had been absolutely no prognosis that her condition would develop with such rapidity. To his initial surprise succeeded a conviction – that not only was something wrong, but it was something very unusual; clearly this woman had suffered a devastating shock of some kind, and was now laboring under severe mental stress. What kind, he had no need to inquire; of the causes he might be ignorant, but he knew disintegrating fear and anxiety when he saw them. All this, flashing upon him in the fraction of a second, was interrupted by Myra's voice. Even that had changed; from light to flirtatious it had become strained and harsh, unrecognizable.

"Are you here," she challenged him instantly, "because that daughter of mine put you up to it?"

"Why should you think that?" he countered soothingly.

"Because she's been after me to see you," Myra answered. "Why won't she let me alone? why won't they all let me alone?"

"Miss Walworth has nothing to do with my coming to see you," declared the doctor. He pitched his voice to quell hers and succeeded –

for the moment. "But if she had, it would be just what she should have done. Anyone can see you're not well, that you've been neglecting yourself —"

"Then she did put you up to it!" Myra interrupted. Her voice was frenzied again, and a fine tremor coursed through her at irregular intervals.

"Now that's enough," he said with authority, astounded at her slitted, suspicious eyes, her peculiar aura of distraction; this suburban matron made him think of a guilt-ridden Borgia. "I'm here on my own, and not because of anyone else. But I'm certainly glad I dropped in." He eyed her severely, with admonition. "I'm surprised at you, neglecting yourself like this — I should think you'd have better sense." She loved, he knew, to be scolded. "You don't feel well, do you? not nearly as well as last time I saw you?"

"I — I suppose not." She was subsiding into sulkiness, he saw with relief; easier to cope with that than with her wild-eyed desperation, at any rate.

"Ann didn't call me," he reproached her, adroitly carrying the war into the enemy's camp. "You don't believe in me any more, do you?"

"That's not it at all," she defended herself;

the mere change from the offensive was something gained.

"You're worried about something," he accused, bluntly.

"How do you know?" she challenged at once, her earlier look of suspicion returning.

"How do I know!? I can see it — a blind man could see it. And I warned you against it, remember? Worry, Mrs. Walworth —" he overbore her as she tried to interrupt, "— worry is your worst enemy just now, it's the one thing you can't stand."

"Well, I have been worried," she admitted, rallying slightly and shooting him a flirtatious look. This, though pitiful enough in view of her ruinous appearance, pleased him immensely; it was so much more her usual style.

"Do you want to talk about it?" he began, then stopped; both were silent as the maid came in with the coffee tray, placed it, and went out again. "If you'd like to," he resumed, "with me or with anyone — so that some way could be found to relieve you —"

"There is no way," Myra interrupted. She licked her lips and shot him another look — between archness and melancholy this time, with a touch of furtiveness thrown in. "The truth is, doctor, I've . . . money worries. I've lost some money, quite a . . . quite a large sum, in fact."

"I see." He did see; the loss of possessions, any kind, would be for a woman of Myra's type the supreme tragedy. "Yes, well, but even if it's a serious loss — is it that serious?"

"At my age —" Myra began; he interrupted. "Serious enough to let it prey on your mind and ruin your health, without your lifting a finger about it? Why didn't you call me, at least?"

"I guess I should have," Myra acknowledged, batting her eyelids with little-girl contrition.

"Should have, but didn't," he accused her. She loved his tone of reproval, she was eating it up. "All right, if you don't love me any more, let me send you to a specialist. There's a first-class one nearby, in Vale Park — Dr. Thompson."

"Oh, no," protested Myra, "you're my doctor."

"Then —" he loomed over her, mock-threatening, "— don't you forget it." By sheer hard labor he had won her from her wild antagonism into the mood he wanted, and the rest of the interview went swimmingly. He examined her, wrote additional prescriptions, arranged for the taking of another cardiogram. To all of this she agreed with coquettish docility, and with evident pleasure watched him dispose of the coffee, also of some sweet and very rich cookies. He detested sweets.

At the moment of his departure, however, he found that her explanation – of money worries – had left him with a lingering doubt; a sense that she had left something unsaid. Cautiously he hazarded one more inquiry.

"Mrs. Walworth, beside what you told me – about the money – is there anything else on your mind?"

Did she hesitate minutely? then answer too rapidly? He could not have sworn with entire certainty to either.

"No, there's nothing on my mind but losing that money," smiled Myra. "Isn't that enough?"

She sounded reasonably frank, and perforce he had to be satisfied.

Going downstairs, Ralph reflected that undoubtedly one of the heavier crosses of medical practice was the cajoling of spoiled old women; it was to be hoped that his patience would not skid fatally one day. A burp caught him unaware; he muttered, "Damn those cookies."

Before letting himself out, he glanced toward the rear hall, Ann's door. It was closed; there was no sound of occupancy. This was just as well, for any hurried colloquy between them now, on the subject of his interview with Myra, was not very practicable in this house.

At the first drugstore he stopped; went in, and called the Walworth number. The maid answered, and informed him that Ann was out.

"No, no message," he returned, to her query. "I'll call again."

He left the booth with an unexpected and illogical feeling of disappointment.

CHAPTER 13

Connie, from across the snowy damask of the Vale Park Country Club, surveyed Theo, over whom bent, in an attentive huddle, the dining-room steward and two waiters. Still the same maddening old fusspot, she reflected; unable to order lunch, even, without making a big production of it. Absenting her mind from their jabbering, she sat back comfortably and began debating various means of approach to the subject that preoccupied her.

"Thick lambchops then, if you've nothing but steer beef," pronounced Theo finally, after exhaustive discussion. "You've fresh asparagus? fresh, mind, not frozen? asparagus then, and plenty of hollandaise. Salad, Connie? no? nor for me either, Martin. We'll order coffee and dessert later."

The steward and waiters began dispersing busily in various directions.

"Wait, wait, Martin." Theo touched the stem of his cocktail glass. "Another, Connie? no?

you're sure? For me then, Martin — just one." As the steward bowed and went away, he pursued, "Sure you won't have another, Connie?"

"Two cocktails before lunch are my limit," Connie assured him.

"Well, sometimes I feel I need it," Theo grumbled. He grumbled habitually, on a note of permanent, wheezy complaint — wheezy because his considerable overweight made him short in the wind. Also, at the moment, he felt a specific, and increasing, resentment — directed at the young woman across the table from him. Somehow she had forced him into this luncheon date, confound her; coerced him, practically, into inviting her, in order to tell him her troubles. Theo dreaded all trouble, his own or other people's, and he shrank from hard-luck stories like a tropical plant from a cold wind. Mentally he began estimating the probable amount of the touch she would try to make, with a fatalistic certainty that this was her ultimate purpose in wanting to see him. Then he began calculating the very least amount that he could, in decency, offer her. At this point he remembered that using the brain at mealtimes was bad for the digestion; by forcing him to use his brain, she was going to spoil his lunch for him. No, she had spoiled it already. By what right, he fumed to himself, did she land on *his* neck in this manner? She was not even a blood-relation; he had no obligation toward her, not the least in the world.

Connie, on the other hand, was engaged in her own appraisal of this connection by marriage. Thoughtfully, if covertly, her eye ranged downward over the scanty hair and low forehead, the vacant eyes, round like a Peke's, the short thick nose, the toothbrush mustache bristling sparsely above heavy pouting lips — all barber-groomed to a high gloss, inhumanly immaculate. His color was unhealthy; more florid than she remembered it, with the purple undercast indicative of too-good living and hovering apoplexy; she estimated that he had gained another ten or twelve pounds since she had last seen him.

"I'll bet he's never had a woman in his life," she thought with contempt. Almost unbelievable, that this mass of pulp had connived at murder; you could see at a glance his cowardice, his quivering dread of anything unpleasant. However, for lack of better, her thesis *must* be that he had been involved with the other three, all those years ago. Her next consideration was, that somehow she must get him to talk about that particular period, however generally or indirectly; he might let fall something, anything; the merest hint might lead to something. And if — her heart sank at the thought — this meeting proved barren, she would be at a loss for her next expedient.

Theo waited, in silence, for his third cocktail, his eyes bent sulkily on the table, his pudgy fingers stirring and jerking spasmodically. At the murmured excuse, the careful hand stealing in front of him to deposit the frosty glass with a clear greenish light in its liquid depths, he came to life.

"Three drinks before lunch're unusual for me too," he half-apologized, after the first greedy swig. "But as a matter of fact, I don't feel too well."

"How do you feel?" she felt obliged to inquire.

"Oh, nothing — a bit seedy." He sucked up the last drops of his cocktail avidly. Then he seemed to revive a little; his popping, bloodshot eyes met hers.

"So Archie handed in his papers," he recapitulated, dolefully. He had no desire to talk about Archie; he was merely trying to stave off the moment of Connie's request for a loan. "The first to go, hah? the first of us four."

"Yes," murmured Connie, scenting in his words a possible lead; she seized on it at once.

"I went to see Luanna — to tell her about Archie," she went on. "Not that she understood, but the old place looks awfully well, you know? they really keep it up very well."

"Do they?" said Theo. "By the way, have you ever eaten at the Trois Couronnes, just outside St. Lo? You've never tasted seafood unless you've been there, I promise you. I wanted sole for lunch today," he pouted. "Just felt like fish — but of course they'd have to use canned mussels in the sauce, so no thanks. Have any good new eating places opened up around here, while I was away?"

She answered mechanically, while her mind weighed his instant digression at her mention of the house; had it been merely accidental, or not? She must wait until a little later, then try again.

Lunch was served, thick succulent chops, lively pale-browned ruched on the edges with lively dark-brown, and huge asparagus, the green spears tenderly laved in pale yellow sauce, smooth as satin. Connie picked and Theo gobbled and began talking about food, the one topic that ever roused him to any semblance of animation; he discoursed of restaurants in Normandy, restaurants in and around Paris, restaurants on the Riviera. By the time the dishes were removed she had decided on her second attempt. She made it.

"Funny, but I never realized how huge Luanna's house really is," she essayed, eyeing him covertly. "The little shack I live in — you could put it into one of the downstairs rooms."

"Always hated the place," he returned, peevishly. "Don't make me talk about it. Well, Martin, what's for dessert? Dessert, Connie? no dessert? you're sure? just coffee? Now all right, Martin, bring some vanilla ice-cream, a half-cup of raisins — got that? — and a double pony of rum, light, mind you, not dark. And warm up a pony of brandy for me — and two demi-tasse. That's all."

Martin glided away, and Connie surveyed Theo, who in silence, and with an oddly worried expression on his face, was breaking lump-sugar into bits. His second refusal to talk about the old place, his undisguised shying-away from the subject, *might* indicate guilty knowledge on his part; but what guilty knowledge? If he ran like a deer at the least introduction of the topic, he could defeat her conclusively. In her mind she said a hopeless farewell to the prospect of getting anything out of him — except this heavy lunch, and she hated large mid-day meals. The ready venom of her nature rose to the surface, and with slant-eyed contempt she sat watching his performance with his dessert, which had now been served. All over the surface of the ice-cream he was scooping little pits with the tip of a spoon; into each hole so made he dropped two or three raisins, topped them off with a bit of lump-sugar, and with tender, minute attention saturated the whole with rum. Then he took the heated brandy from Martin, lit it, and poured it over the ice-cream. At once the whole thing was polka-dotted with fire; the sugar sizzled, bubbled down into crusty little roofs over the raisins; a breath of blue flame trembled over the suave cream, melting it slightly, and was gone. Theo watched with absorbed delight.

"My own idea," he said proudly, picking up his spoon. However, when the concoction was only half-dispatched, his gusto seemed to wane; the worried look was back on his face, intensified.

"Archie," he said glumly, without preamble, "was only three years older'n I am."

"Is that so?" returned Connie, with careful disinterest, but beneath it alert once more at this mention of one of the principals.

"I tell you, when the others begin dropping off — well, it makes you think." His round eyes were fixed on her lugubriously; his florid color seemed less florid. "This dying business —

never thought about it much before. Of course all this nonsense about an after-life — the Judgment — punishment — nobody believes that stuff any more." He seemed to be reassuring himself. "Sunday school stories." He uttered a hoarse laugh, sudden and forced, then stopped as suddenly, sighed, and rubbed his eyes. "Haven't been any too well lately," he complained again; then, to the hovering steward, "Take this dam' thing away, Martin — makes me sick to look at it."

As the ruined mess of raisins, sugar and ice-cream was whisked away, "But just what's the matter with you?" Connie inquired, putting out the most delicate of feelers — for he seemed to be getting at something, in his sluggish way.

He took a moment to answer; then, "Well, it's those awful nights, mostly." He sat stirring and stirring his thimbleful of black coffee, looking down into it as into a fathomless depth. "Fact is," he confided to the coffee-cup, "fact is — these five, six weeks — I've been having night-mares."

"Nightmares?" echoed Connie, with a quickening sense of having heard this before.

"Or a nightmare, rather — always about the same thing," sighed Theo. His color had faded still more; he looked unhealthily replete with lunch, tight to bursting. "Keep dreaming I'm in a car, taking a ride with Lu and the nurse."

"What nurse?" said Connie, suddenly dizzy with premonition. He was on the verge of revealing the very thing she wanted; she knew it, in some occult fashion. All of her drew into one taut, painfully-listening ear.

"Mamma's nurse," returned Theo. "I don't mean our own mother's, I mean — you know — Margaret's. Well, in this dream I'm driving with Lu and that Mrs. Schermerhorn — always driving, driving, with Lu and Mrs. Schermerhorn."

"That doesn't sound like a nightmare," said Connie, making herself talk calmly over her heart-racketing excitement. "Why should it upset you?"

"It's upsetting in the dream," mumbled Theo, talking to himself rather than to her. "Because I know it'll go on and on forever — I'll go on driving, Mrs. Schermerhorn'll go on talking. Like on the day she died — our step-mother, I mean. I'd taken the nurse and Lu for a little spin, not more'n a half-hour, and when we got back she'd passed away in the meantime — just died in that half-hour," he concluded, and again revolved the spoon in his untasted coffee.

"But she was old, wasn't she?" Connie asked. Her heart was pounding so violently she could hardly get the words out. "Wasn't she very old?"

He seemed not to hear, only replying to her question with another; a harking-back to an earlier topic.

"You don't believe there's an after-life, do you, Connie?" he almost pleaded, fixing his eyes on her with a curious distress and entreaty. "All that rot?"

"I've never thought about it," shrugged Connie. "I don't believe anyone believes in it much, any more."

"No, I suppose not," sighed Theo. But he sagged another degree, seeming to take no comfort from her opinion, then heavily signaled Martin, to Connie's wild relief; she was mad to get away, to be alone, to evaluate her new findings, to add and calculate. She waited through an eternity as Theo signed the check, transmitted an affable message to the chef, and otherwise dawdled, then said good-bye and left hastily, not even — to Theo's astonishment and relief — having made the slightest attempt at a touch. Almost running to her convertible, she started it with a roar and was off, racing across the miles that separated her from the gatehouse.

In her small living-room, she tore off her things, threw herself into a chair, and sat for some time in a movelessness almost cataleptic. Then she rose and retrieved Archie's diary from its hiding-place. When she had re-read the long entry, she laid it down slowly, her eyes fixed on distance.

We went downstairs and waited for the others, and for the nurse . . . now it made sense, in the light of what Theo had revealed; they had taken measures to get rid of the nurse during the crucial period — of the murder itself.

And if this were still only a theory, yet Theo, unconsciously, had placed in her hands the means of substantiating it. Comical, his sudden fears and speculation about life after death; the origin of his terrors was easy to divine, knowing what she knew — or almost knew. The slightest smile moved the corners of her mouth. And even more comical, at this late date, to be on the track of a murder whose perpetrators must feel safer than safe. . . . Better not smile too soon, she admonished herself; she still had a lot of ground to cover. But her lips still curved secretively as she reached for the local telephone directory and turned to the classified section.

Five minutes later she stood at Lydia's phone and commenced dialing the first number of the short list she had made — only five names in all. When a voice answered, she inquired briskly, "Keystone Nurses' Registry? . . . Have you a nurse on your lists by the name of Schermerhorn — a nurse named Mrs. Schermerhorn?"

CHAPTER 14

"Hello?" said Ann.

"Is this Miss Walworth?"

At the voice that came over the phone, her heart struck her ribs one hard blow, then started racing madly.

"Yes, Dr. Markham," she answered composedly.

"I called you before — almost a week ago," he went on. "Sorry I've let it slide 'til now, but I've been swamped. Well, I saw your mother — and spoke to her."

"Yes?" Her voice quickened.

"Yes, and in a way you were right. Her condition has deteriorated to a certain degree, and you were quite right in telling me."

"Is she much worse?"

"Not too much — I've her new cardiogram, and whatever's developed, we can check pretty well. The main thing is, of course, that she should be relieved of her sense of strain."

"Did you talk to her about that?" demanded Ann.

"Oh yes — she's been under a strain. You were right about that too."

"Did she say what it was?"

"Yes, she talked about it — she was perfectly open about it."

"What was the trouble?" Ann breathed. Apprehension dried her mouth and tightened her breathing.

"Money worries — she's been having serious money worries."

"Is *that* what she told you!" she demanded with unbelief.

"Why yes." He sounded slightly taken aback.

"That's just ridiculous," she said bluntly. "She wasn't telling you the truth."

"I didn't have that impression, Miss Walworth."

"That I can't help," she retorted. "Did she say what kind of money worries?"

"Well, she wouldn't, would she — to me?"

"Did she mention Mrs. Walworth?" she persisted. "Did she say anything at all about Connie?"

"Not a word," said the doctor firmly.

"Then she was lying to you, don't you see!" she expostulated, feeling as though she battered an uncaring stone wall. "It's all

163

Connie — the whole trouble's Connie!"

"Now, now —" he was objectionably patient and soothing, "— if Mrs. Walworth were at the bottom of the trouble — or any part of it, even — wouldn't your mother have told me?"

The question brought her to a full stop; she considered it with growing perplexity and indecision.

"I don't know," she admitted finally. "It depends on what the trouble between them is. No, I haven't the least idea —" she hated it, sounding so ineffectual, "— whether she'd tell you about it or not."

"Has Mrs. Walworth visited your mother recently?"

"Not for ten days," she answered, spiritless. "I've been sticking close to home, so I know."

"Well then —" he was so reasonable as to be disgusting "— if she doesn't come around any more, the situation — the little flare-up, whatever it was — seems to be over, don't you think so?"

"I don't think anything of the kind," she retorted. "*She* may not be around, but whatever she started is still going on. You only have to look at Mamma to see it."

"Well, whenever you can give me something more concrete to go on . . ." His tone indicated that he was about to terminate the conversation, and she was silent a moment, balked and angry.

"Yes," she answered coldly. "I should have had something much more definite for you, shouldn't I? I'm sorry to have taken your time." In her heart she relinquished him totally as a source of help; whatever was going to be done about the situation would be done by herself. "But thank you for calling me, doctor. Goodbye."

"Just a moment, Miss Walworth," he said hastily — to his own surprise. All at once he wanted to know something about this girl; he cast about hastily and came up with a plausible inquiry. "Ah — tell me, have you ever done any hospital work, by chance? of any kind?"

"Such as nurse's-aiding?" she returned. "No, I'm just a commercial chemist. I specialized in plastics."

"Is that so." His quickened interest fell pleasantly on her ears. "Are you working at it now?"

"No." The pang was there, only a little less keen than at first. "My brother died, and I gave up my job and came home."

"That was a mistake," he half-stated, half-asked.

"I know," she admitted. "But at the time,

165

there didn't seem anything else to do."

"Could you adapt yourself to a hospital laboratory, do you think?"

"Why —" she hesitated, frowning. "Not without a couple of years' extra study, I shouldn't think."

"We're alarmingly short of laboratory help at Hargesville Memorial," he pursued. "You're a trained person — you could use some of your technics in a different field, and catch up on the rest. If you ever decide to do anything about it, come talk to me, won't you? We could —"

"Dr. Markham," she interrupted him, in dismay. The sound of a motor had come to her ears, then Myra's car flashed past the living-room windows. "Mamma's just coming home," she explained. "She'd better not find me talking to you."

"Maybe not," he agreed hastily. "Goodbye. Remember, though."

"I'll remember," said Ann, and hung up with mixed emotions. That she should have to cut him short the first, the very first time he had shown any inclination to talk to her; her heart bled at her perverse bad luck. On the other hand, he had opened to her the prospect of seeing him, of being with him, however briefly. . . . She went to open the rear hall door, which Myra was approaching over the flagstone walk.

"What an expression," was Myra's salutation, as she came through. "Perfect for a funeral." But she said it not unamiably, and Ann returned, "It's going to waste then, too bad," and went upstairs at her mother's heels, noting that she ascended much more slowly than was her wont. Once in her room, Myra let herself be helped off with her coat; then, with her hat still on, she slumped into a chair and made no further move. At each corner of her mouth hung a fold of skin, a sort of pleat, that had never been there before — at least not noticeably so.

"Make me a drink, will you?" she said. "A short one — rye."

"Why not a cup of tea?" Ann wheedled. "So much better for you."

"If I've got to live that way — on things that're good for me — I'd rather kick off," said Myra. "Oh, all right, tea then. Bring it up here."

"I was going to," said Ann, already making for the door.

"Wait," said Myra suddenly. With an effort, and a strengthless look, she was raising herself from her chair. Going to her dressing-table, she unlocked a drawer, and from it took a sturdy leather case.

"These are for you," she said abruptly.

Ann, stunned, looked down at the flashing, glittering mass, from which her eye disentangled, as more familiar to her, the sapphire clip and the two big solitaires.

"Why . . . what . . ." she began to stammer.

"I haven't had any of these things on for three or four years now," said Myra. "These are all I ever wear." She raised both hands, on which sparkled the double hoop of her wedding-ring, a beautiful marquise, and a very good emerald. "And this." She touched the pin at her throat.

"But I don't dress up to things like that," said Ann, in protest and dismay. "I don't go places where I could wear them —"

"Then start dressing up to them!" Myra interrupted with asperity. "I don't care how brainy you are, it's no excuse for slouching around the way you do. Get yourself some good clothes — get out and around, make some kind of a show, for God's sake! I want you to have them now, while you're young, not when you've got a fifty-year-old neck! Take them!" she commanded, thrusting it at Ann. "Take them."

"I don't want them," said Ann stubbornly.

"Don't make me argue!" With this formula,

which she used frequently and unscrupulously, Myra always quelled any difference of opinion. "Take them downstairs. And here —" she reached into her bag, withdrew an envelope, "— its a deed of gift, just in case — so there can't be any disputes or funny business over it. Keep it in a safe place. Now go along with you," she urged fretfully. "Don't make me wear myself out talking."

In silence Ann took the envelope and box of jewelry, and went with them toward the door.

Downstairs, in melancholy abstraction, she considered the box of valuable gewgaws. Nowhere on her immediate horizon could she perceive occasions for wearing jewelry of such value, and the worry far outweighed any pleasure or use she might get out of them. Get a safe-deposit box, she thought; shut them up uselessly, in the dark. Then her thoughts turned to Myra's generosity, her lethal generosity. This consisted of giving you what she wanted you to have; never, by any chance, what you yourself wanted.

CHAPTER 15

Connie, with complacency, surveyed her luncheon guest. Not so much her guest, as her quarry; and a quarry it had taken her three weeks to run down. First the woman had been on a case, then she had gone directly onto another case, but here she was at last, in the flesh — ample flesh — captured for lunch at the most expensive country restaurant that Connie could think of in the vicinity. She surveyed the red, foolishly good-natured face, in itself almost a guarantee of volubility, and was intensely grateful that she had not run up against one of the silent, reserved ethical type.

"Well, this is certainly lovely," commented Mrs. Schermerhorn. Her gaze devoured the room, with its massive beams overhead, its crackling fire in the huge fireplace, its gleaming bar. Delicious smells floated on the air; smartly-jacketed waiters moved to and fro; there was a well-bred conversational hum of voices. "Lovely," she repeated. "It just goes to show the nice things you can do if you have the wherewith."

"I'm *so* glad you like it," Connie smirked, mentally estimating that it might be unwise to offer the old cow a third martini. She was already working on her second, and Connie wanted her loosened-up and nicely talkative — but dependably talkative, not irresponsibly so.

"Shall we order now?" she suggested. "They do a wonderful chafing-dish thing here, lobster and shrimp. Do you like that?"

"Do I not!" said Mrs. Schermerhorn archly. When the order had been given, she said feelingly, "It's lovely of you to take me here, Mrs. Walworth, just lovely. I've been working so hard, and it's such *mean* work sometimes, nursing — so I'm getting a great big lift out of this, let me tell you. Well, cheers."

"Pay dirt in your eye," said Connie. "And I'm so glad I could locate you, Mrs. Schermerhorn. I understand you did such a wonderful job when old Mrs. Gedney was ill — she was my mother-in-law's step-mother, you see — so I thought, seeing my mother-in-law might need a nurse pretty soon, it might be a good idea to contact you." For this was the fiction that Connie had devised as the excuse for seeking this interview.

"I remember Mrs. Walworth quite well,

though I only saw her a few times," said Mrs. Schermerhorn. "Very pretty, I always thought, with that lovely red hair. Too bad she's sick — I'm sorry to hear it. By the way," she queried, with a slight frown, "is she bedridden?"

"Oh no," said Connie.

"That's good," said Mrs. Schermerhorn. "Of course old Mrs. Gedney was, entirely so, and that makes it very hard. I don't know that I'd be up to a really hard case any more, seeing that I'm not any younger than I was."

"Well, Myra's up and around," Connie assured her. "She's beginning to have some pain though. I was wondering if she had the same thing as old Mrs. Gedney. Do you remember that case distinctly?"

"Do I not," said Mrs. Schermerhorn. She bridled faintly, for some unexplained reason, and looked significant. "Well, of course I don't know your mother-in-law's diagnosis or her symptoms, but if she can hold out as long as Mrs. Gedney, she needn't worry. Eight-four years old!" She took a swallow of martini. "And responded so *well* to medication! It was certainly a surprise when she went off like that, let me tell you."

"Well, but eighty-four years old . . ." Connie demurred.

"Yes, but let me tell you," said Mrs. Schermerhorn. "She'd been getting intravenous shots of B-12. That's routine nowadays, but back in '43 it was a new treatment, you might say experimental. Dr. — what was that doctor's name? well, I'll remember later. But she'd been going downhill fast — you could see it from day to day — so the doctor ordered her those shots as a sort of last resort, I guess it was. And right away, she began picking up."

"*Did* she?"

"Marvelously," affirmed Mrs. Schermerhorn. "And of course the doctor was just tickled pink. He said she might very well live to ninety or over, and it looked it — the general increase of strength was so remarkable. For instance, she worked up a tremendous appetite. She'd have a great big breakfast, and a meat luncheon, and a perfectly enormous dinner — why, that little thread of a woman, you didn't know where she put it all. And *wanted* her food — anxious for it."

Connie's mind flicked back to that significant passage, in the will; by its light she could well understand the hatred Myra must have felt for this indestructible old lady, with her improvement, her big appetite, her tenacity of life — indecent. "Then what happened?" she inquired with unfeigned interest.

"Well, she just kept on improving," said

Mrs. Schermerhorn, "until that particular day – Oh dear, that day."

"Yes?" Connie murmured negligently, knotted all over with tension.

"Well, Mrs. Walworth had driven around with her two brothers to see Mrs. Gedney – I forget the brothers' names – and right away she noticed I looked tired, she was always very nice to me. Well, I *was* tired, no question about it. You see, it was the maid's day off, with just the cook down in the kitchen, but you couldn't ask *her* to do anything – not her. Of course that daughter – that Louella or whoever – she lived there too, but she was worse than useless. So that left me all alone to cope with the old lady, and she was very difficult and keyed-up that day, my, she was a handful. Do this, do that, do the other – and it was all up to me, and the *stairs* in that huge house, and the *distances!* Well, by the time your mother-in-law showed up it was around two in the afternoon, and the patient, she'd had her lunch and dozed off, praise be. And by that time I was fagged-out, let me tell you, I was ready to drop."

"I should think so," sympathized Connie.

"Well –" Mrs. Schermerhorn, under this flattering warmth and attention, expanded visibly, like a middle-aged rose. "Well, Mrs. Walworth said I looked worn-out, and why didn't I go out and have a little drive, to rest me."

"I see," said Connie. The same premonitory excitement as with Theo was quivering through her, gaining in strength by the moment.

"She said one of her brothers would drive me, and the other brother would wait there with her, until I came back. I said no, I oughtn't, and she said, why couldn't I for just a half-hour or so, and she'd look in on the old lady every so often. But I knew the patient would probably sleep the better part of an hour, and it was a gorgeous summer day, so I let myself be tempted." She sighed, stopped.

"Yes?" Connie prompted gently, afraid that a single pause, unduly extended, would fatally weaken the thread.

"I went," said Mrs. Schermerhorn. "Louella — was that her name, by the way?"

"Luanna."

"I knew it was something like that. Well, Luanna went along too, and the brother drove us, the short fat one, what's *his* name —?"

"Theodore," said Connie, through all-but-clenched teeth; damn the old fool's digressions and interruptions.

"Theodore? now him I don't remember so well. But the three of us went out, just for this

175

little short spin, and got back well within the half-hour. And *when* we got back ..." she paused again.

"Yes?" breathed Connie.

The waiter approached, wheeling a table on which stood plates and a burnished chafing-dish. With grandiloquent gestures, as if performing before a public, he lifted the copper lid, stirred the contents, flamed them, then served; huge sauce-drenched portions of orange-red, with bits of blue flame still lurking in their valleys. Supplementary plates, loaded with beautiful salad, were placed on the table.

"Well!" beamed Mrs. Schermerhorn. She forked up some pilaff, doused it well into the sauce, transfixed a big chunk of lobster and put the whole in her mouth. Then she closed her eyes and went perfectly rigid, in a catalepsy of appreciation.

"Mmmmhhh!" she moaned, as though in pain. *"Mmmmhhh!"* She took another loaded forkful. *"Never,"* she enunciated, "have I tasted *anything* like it."

Connie, beneath her hostessy simper, was in agony. The waiter's interruption could not have come at a worse moment; she must get the woman back onto her trolley, and do it without conspicuous pressure or anxiety. "They do have good food here, don't they?" she said lightly.

"Good!" said Mrs. Schermerhorn, scornfully underlining the inadequacy of this word, then slowly and deliberately savored another mouthful, with her eyes half-closed.

"I'm so glad you like it," Connie gushed.

"Like it," pronounced Mrs. Schermerhorn, "is not the word." Her questing fork gathered up another load, prior to delivery. "Now let's see, about old Mrs. Gedney — where was I?"

"You'd been out for a ride and come back," said Connie, with unbounded relief.

"Or maybe," her guest queried anxiously, "you'd rather not spoil this gorgeous food with talking about disagreeable things?"

"I don't mind, if you don't," Connie shrugged. "You tell it so well I was very interested."

"In that case —" beamed Mrs. Schermerhorn, and broke off. "Now let's see what the salad's like." There followed a process not unlike the delivery of a bale of hay into a haymow. "Oh, it's wonderful. What's that stuff sprinkled over it?"

"Marjoram or basil, maybe."

"Aren't you going to eat yours?" queried Mrs. Schermerhorn, anxiously.

"I don't think so," said Connie, "I've had it here before, and I don't eat a very big lunch. You were saying —" she hazarded, delicately.

"Oh yes, about Mrs. Gedney. Well, we came back." Mrs. Schermerhorn embarked once more on her narrative. "I went up to her room – as soon as I'd laid off my hat – and peeked in. She seemed to be asleep. Well, I was just about to close the door again, when it struck me that . . . that . . . well I don't know just what *did* strike me, maybe it was too quiet in the room or maybe, unconsciously, I couldn't see or hear any breathing –"

Connie nodded.

"– so I went up to the bed – and my dear, she was gone. Well, you could have knocked me over with a feather! There'd been absolutely no indication – I mean, she'd been doing so very *well!* –"

"How did she look?" inquired Connie, with a purpose in so doing. "Could you tell what had happened, or –"

"She looked absolutely peaceful," said Mrs. Schermerhorn. "There was no sign of anything, I mean, sometimes when there's a seizure the body's contorted – but there was nothing like that in this case, she just lay there looking perfectly natural."

"What did you do?"

"I called the doctor," said Mrs. Schermerhorn. She impaled lettuce with sudden, angry thrusts of the fork. "He came at once, and, well

– he blew up. Insulting, that's what he was."
She stabbed more lettuce, as if it were the
doctor. "You'd think I'd poisoned the old lady
instead of going out for a breath of air that God
knows I needed – and even if I'd been there
when she went off, what could I have done?"

"Didn't Mrs. Walworth notice anything
wrong?" asked Connie, smoothly.

"How could she? she was downstairs with
her brother most of the time," returned Mrs.
Schermerhorn. "Excuse me if I talk and eat,
but it's all so *delish!* – No, Mrs. Walworth was
just as shocked as I was – they were all
shocked. She said she'd looked in on her less
than ten minutes before, and she seemed to be
asleep. – What was the other brother's name,
again – the one that waited at the house with
Mrs. Walworth?"

"Archie."

"That's the one," said Mrs. Schermerhorn. "I
thought he was very nice, so refined-looking.
How is he?"

"Dead," said Connie. "About six weeks ago."

"Tss!" sighed the other. "But there, we all
come to it, don't we? But I thought he was
very, very nice."

"What else happened – when the doctor
came?" asked Connie, fighting her veering
craft back on course.

"He was horrible. He was just an old bully, I always hated that Dr. Peters —" she broke off triumphantly. "— that's his name, Dr. Peters, I knew I'd remember —" she broke off again, and eyed Connie with speculation. "A little while ago," she said thoughtfully, "you said I'd done a wonderful job with Mrs. Gedney. Who told you that, may I ask?"

"The family." Connie produced a specific witness who could certainly not refute her. "Archie, especially."

"I'm glad someone thought so," averred Mrs. Schermerhorn, darkly, "because there were those who didn't."

"How do you mean?"

"Well, the doctor raised Ned about a mark on Mrs. Gedney's forearm," explained Mrs. Schermerhorn. "You see, she'd been getting so very many shots, and sometimes, in that case, you're likely to get that heavy mottling under the skin, like black-and-blue marks, and some of the punctures might bleed a little, well — I'd just given her her intravenous before she went to sleep, and the doctor claimed I'd bungled it because of this big mark — and I *had* punched her there, but I hadn't noticed anything out of the way — but sometimes, as I say, it might bleed a little, which wasn't my fault — but the way he *talked!*" Her cheeks, flushed with eating, took on a richer stain of reminiscent indignation. "Did you know —" she breathed conspiratorially, leaning across the table toward Connie "— did you know there was an autopsy?"

"No," said Connie, genuinely startled; this was a bombshell.

"I wasn't supposed to know it," said Mrs. Schermerhorn, "but I heard, indirectly."

"Did they find anything?" asked Connie, focussed on the other with the most unaffected intentness.

"Not that I ever heard," said her vis-à-vis. "And if they had, why of course it would have been in the papers. *Naturally* they wouldn't find anything. Just imagine," she exclaimed indignantly "— *imagine* demanding an autopsy in a fine wealthy family like the Gedneys, as if they were tenement people or criminals or something! Scandalous — but it was like that Dr. Peters. Just bound to stir up trouble if he could, the old boor." She pursued, cornered, and dispatched the last morsels on her plate, then sat back triumphant and exclaimed, "Well, that's the best meal *I* ever had, I don't mind telling you."

"I'm so glad you liked it," said Connie, in a divided frame of mind. The old gasbag had come through nobly with some invaluable details, but the thought of the unsuccessful autopsy was disturbing; an inexplicable piece in the slowly-forming jigsaw. The gasbag had nothing more to offer, she was sure; she had an air of being through with the subject. "What do you like for dessert?" she inquired.

"Well, I shouldn't, but —" Mrs. Schermerhorn pondered the chalked slate presented by the waiter. "— I think — that mocha roll with whipped cream."

"And coffee — and have a cordial," urged Connie. "Waiter, two benedictines."

"Well, pop my girdle!" ejaculated Mrs. Schermerhorn, riotously. "This is a field day for sure."

They parted on terms of the extremest cordiality.

"Now if Mrs. Walworth ever needs me," said Mrs. Schermerhorn, as Connie set her down in front of a small dark apartment house, "I'd be glad to come."

"I'm so glad I know about you," said Connie.

"And thanks a million for lunch."

"It was fun," smiled Connie.

"More fun for me than *you'll* ever know," the other assured her. "But remember, in case you need me, I'd certainly do my best for your mother-in-law."

As Connie drove away, she thought ribaldly, "I'll do my best for my mother-in-law, too, nursie."

CHAPTER 16

"Why haven't you gotten those new clothes yet?" Myra demanded.

"I'm going to," Ann assured her. "Any day now."

And the reminder — for she had virtually forgotten about it — was by no means unpleasant, after nearly a month of close confinement to the house, in readiness to intercept an ill-boding visitor. Suddenly she was sick to death of being cooped up; she owed herself a holiday of some kind, even if it only consisted of sailing out and embellishing herself a little. For nearly a month, as far as she knew, there had been no sign of Connie, and her waiting tension had eased off little by little, imperceptibly. Could it have been, even, as the doctor suggested? that she had heard some trifling fracas, and had blown it up out of all proportion? She half-accepted, half-rejected this theory, alternately. Myra's scream still ripped through her inner ear, but less vividly by far, less shockingly. What if she had simply been mistaken about the whole thing, like a fool?

"Well, what're you waiting for?" Myra was complaining. "Why don't you get them?"

"Tomorrow," Ann said conclusively. "Tomorrow I'll really tear loose." She smiled with a sudden access of lightheartedness. The shadow had passed, perhaps had never existed. Myra was looking undeniably better, almost her old self, in fact, with her careful make-up (heavier than previously, it was true), very smart clothes, and trim red curls — for she had rallied to the point of having her hair dyed, as usual. To be sure Ann sensed, rather than perceived, a darkness of mood that still hung over her, evincing itself in sudden asperities and sharp corners of temper, unlike her usual blandness and smiling composure; but the improvement was patently there. And it was a lovely day, the most marvelous December day, and she was going to get some new clothes. Suddenly she was crazy to get out and about, to breathe fresh air, to drive off somewhere, anywhere. Her heart curvetted absurdly; a surge of wonderful and illogical hope rose within her, and she smiled again. Then she noticed that Myra was eyeing her.

"Looking off into the distance and smiling to

yourself," she commented, with a not-unfriendly malice. "Are you in love?"

"I can look off into the distance and not be in love," Ann retorted. "I can smile and not be in love, either."

"Well —" Myra rose, started to drift out of the room, "— get yourself a fur coat while you're about it, why don't you? A sports fur, beaver or something. It'll be my Christmas present."

Connie stirred finally, after a long, almost unnatural immobility. These preoccupied trances took her frequently nowadays; she was always brooding, calculating, with Archie's diary before her, a reference by which to check her progress. The newly-exhumed fact of the post-mortem had come as a staggering surprise, almost toppling, for the moment, the whole fabric of her murder theory. The older members of the family had kept this secret well; not the slightest reference to it had ever reached Connie's ears. Now there confronted her the principal enigma; if the old lady's corpse had been autopsied and had revealed nothing — of what, then, was Myra afraid? But she was afraid; her reaction to the first blackmail attempt had told Connie that. Her behavior on this occasion had also revealed her, somehow, as having directed and generaled the plan from the first. But that Myra — Myra of all people — had been smart enough to beat an autopsy: preposterous. She considered this unlikely fact until she felt her mind a void, stale and fatigued with speculation. Better give it up for awhile; go out for a turn, talk to Lydia a few minutes. . . .

Lydia was not in the house, or — when Connie explored — in the workshop. The room, cluttered as usual, was empty; on the table stood a wooden rack of ten cc. hypodermics. Connie's eyes went to them as steel to the magnet, and clung. A stillness wrapped itself around her. Again she had that half-formed, teasing sense of something forgotten, just beyond her grasp . . . after a pause, she emerged from the trance in a state of revelation. Now she knew what instrument Myra had used to commit murder; she knew, not with her intelligence, but with a certainty beyond intelligence. Instantly, though, she doubted again, and the doubt had become full-fledged between the time that she left the workshop and regained her own living-room.

Again she sat down, ignoring the diary (by the way, she was crazy to leave it around like that, she must be more careful in future) and pushed everything out of her mind; everything but the one task of putting herself in Myra's place, of retracing Myra's steps, twelve years ago.

She was Myra; she was going to commit murder; she was going to use a hypodermic. At this point, Connie ran up against the first major obstacle. The hypodermic, so glibly mentioned in fiction, as easy, apparently, to come by; but if you were an ordinary person without gang or criminal connections, where, actually, could you obtain a hypodermic? From a drugstore? a medical supply house? *Please, Mr. Mattern, I want a hypodermic.* She could imagine the local druggist's reaction to that one; that old busybody, with his inquisitive little grey eyes. *A hypodermic, Mrs. Walworth?* And at this point, her imagined dialogue broke down. Were the things sold to anyone over the counter, like bandages or aspirin? She doubted it; she doubted it extremely. In any case, what a peculiar request, attention-attracting; almost as much so as an attempt to buy poison, therefore equally dangerous, in the long run.

Then, in her perplexity, she remembered that she now possessed a gusher of information, and reached for the phone. Mrs. Schermerhorn's cordiality, when she announced herself, almost boiled over, requiring a couple of minutes to subside. Then Connie said archly, "Mrs. Schermerhorn, I'm in a bit of a mess — no, it's not my mother-in-law, it's something else. Well, it's this. You see, I rent a house from this girl who's a sort of veterinarian, I mean she runs a kennel and so forth — and this morning, in her office, I broke one of her hypodermics. I feel so awkward about it because of course I had no business touching it, I picked it up out of curiosity and just dropped it — well, of course I want to replace it, and I haven't the least idea how to do it. How," she ended on an ingenuous little trill of laughter, "— how does one buy a hypodermic?"

"One doesn't," said Mrs. Schermerhorn succinctly. "It would be so much simpler if you just gave her the money — just gave her the price of it."

"But," Connie objected, "you see, I wanted to replace it without her knowing, and I was wondering how —"

"I honestly don't believe —" Mrs. Schermerhorn began, in dubious accents.

"A druggist wouldn't sell me one, would he?" Connie broke in.

"Oh no — not without a doctor's prescription." The answer, decisive, confirmed her earlier supposition. "I imagine I could buy one, though I shouldn't. What size hypodermic was it, Mrs. Walworth?"

"Size?" Connie echoed blankly. "Are there different sizes?"

"Why, bless you," chuckled Mrs. Schermerhorn, benignly enjoying Connie's innocence. "they go all the way from five cc. to the big intravenous ones a hundred cc., two hundred cc. Different sizes! I should say so. By the way, talking of hypodermics," she went on, "I just this minute remembered something else about that disgusting Dr. Peters — in connection with what we were talking about yesterday, you know?"

Connie knew.

"Well, I got back at him on one count, anyway," said Mrs. Schermerhorn vindictively. "On top of everything else, he was carrying on about a hypodermic he'd missed — I forgot all about it 'til now. Isn't it funny, how things come back?"

"The doctor missed a hypodermic?" queried Connie. She spoke with peculiar gentleness, while a sudden, almost painful excitement jumped all along her nerves.

"One of his own, too," averred Mrs. Schermerhorn, "and that's where I got back on him a little, anyway. I told him, 'Well, doctor, none of the hypodermics you gave *me* are missing,' I said. 'There they all are in the rack, every last one of them,' Oh, I told him, all right."

"Where did he miss it from?" asked Connie.

"Don't ask me! from his bag, I suppose. And having the gall to criticize *me!* Fine thing for a doctor to mislay, a hypodermic. Well now, Mrs. Walworth, about this one you've broken —"

"Mrs. Schermerhorn," Connie broke in, "on second thought, I'd better do as you say — just give Lydia the price of it. I wouldn't know how to tell you the size, or anything — I don't know enough about it." She hung up as quickly as possible, in a state of wild jubilation.

A stolen hypodermic. That item closed a gap, supplied a missing link. The gasbag had come through with an extra dividend — and what a dividend! For, instantly, on her mention of it, that elusive, half-remembered something assumed definite shape in Connie's mind.

Luanna. She saw Luanna's face again as it peered up at her from the pillow, with that senseless terror; she heard the thin, wailing voice . . . saying what, exactly? Those broken words and half-phrases, which she had taken for the wanderings of senility, if only she had *listened,* if only she had not been so anxious to tell her news about Archie and escape . . . what was it Luanna had said?

You made me steal it, Myra . . . the doctor . . .

sharp, sharp! . . . the needle . . . but now it made plenty of meaning; and the meaning made sense. Myra *had* been up against the problem of securing the means of murder; she had been far too astute (as Connie had thought) to draw attention to herself by the attempted purchase of such a commodity. Therefore she had put Luanna up to stealing one from old Mrs. Gedney's doctor — and Luanna had succeeded. This Dr. Peters had probably paid frequent visits to the old lady; once or twice out of so many occasions, his bag would inevitably be unattended for a few minutes — say in the downstairs hall, if he used the lavatory, or anything like that. (Her familiarity with the terrain, Connie found, was also paying off.) She nodded to herself, feeling the pleasant tightness of excitement in her chest; yes, it was assuming more and more definite shape, the new elements dovetailing with the old with encouraging smoothness and logic. Also, she knew Myra's reason for choosing that particular means. The old lady received many shots, the nurse had said; among the numerous evidences of this, how inconspicuous, how unlikely of detection, an additional mark!

At this point, both her reconstruction, and her satisfaction, received the same old setback — two setbacks, in fact. First, *what* could Myra have used in the hypodermic? the mysterious agent that had left no trace to tell its tale in the autopsy?

She picked up the diary; scanned a sentence. *How did she do it?*

Here Connie found herself solidly at one with Archie, not only in mystification, but in denying to Myra the capacity for any secret means of murder. Myra and unknown drugs — ridiculous. (*Ridiculous* was not precisely the word Connie used.) Second, with the knowledge of the unsuccessful autopsy behind her, why had she not snapped her fingers at Connie's very first blackmail attempt?

Connie pondered long and intensely over that one before the answer dawned on her, out of her own facile predisposition to evil. Her mother-in-law still feared that silent witness, the old lady's corpse, because . . . *there might be something to discover if they looked again, this time on a new lead.* Even if it were only a probability, it was not reassuring. (It would scare the pants off *me*, Connie acknowledged to herself.)

She devoted another few moments to speculating on Myra's obvious fear of a new autopsy, and on what the lethal hypodermic had contained, and at last gave up; she was no doctor. But aside from these two impenetrable aspects of the affair, Connie had the exultant impatience an athlete must have when he feels himself trained to a knife-edge and ready for the contest. Now she had plenty on the ball; now, if ever, she was equipped for a second demand on Myra.

CHAPTER 17

As soon as Ann went through Bossert's chased and frosted glass doors, she felt better than she had for weeks. The carpet was thick underfoot, the air faintly pervaded with delicious perfume; on all sides was the agreeable modulated stir of prosperous women shopping. Ann sniffed the atmosphere voluptuously, and took an elevator to the third floor.

This region was a world apart; acres of grey carpet and chill elegance, almost unpeopled. Here and there an infrequent figure moved, far away; the very silence sounded expensive. A young woman came forward ingratiatingly as Ann stepped from the elevator, and to her knowledgeable guidance Ann surrendered herself with pleasurable submissiveness. Almost before she knew it she was standing in her undies; the saleswoman was entering the fitting-cubicle with an armful of excitement on hangers.

"Now this —" she was disengaging one,

"— since you're thinking of a suit —"

Two minutes later the full-length mirror gave back the image of a young peeress in a suit whose every line proclaimed its English tailoring. Of soft, misty blue, underscored here and there with darker blue suede, it emphasized her figure and gave her eyes, skin and hair a peculiar lustre; she stared at herself, undisguisedly entranced.

"As soon as I saw you, I thought of this one," said the saleswoman, behind her. "But perhaps you'd like to try on some of the others —"

"Oh *no!*" interrupted Ann, with a monosyllable repudiating "the others" totally. "This is the one. It couldn't be better, could it?"

"No, it could not," agreed the other girl. "It's a dream on you, a perfect dream." Not for nothing was Miss Una Michaels the best saleswoman on the floor.

"I'll take it, please," said Ann. She had not even asked the price, and she would not; she felt deliciously lightheaded. Another piece of delirium, even more uplifting, came into her mind. "A coat," she said. "Could you show me a fur coat — sports?"

"Furs are on the ground floor, Miss," said Una, "but you wait here anyway — just a couple of minutes." She slipped out of the cubicle, leaving Ann to the almost unbelieving contemplation of the blue girl in the mirror. Just clothes could do all that, she marvelled; just clothes. It seemed absurd, and preposterously unfair.

Una was back; behind her was another girl, her arms piled high with coats.

"Miss Oleberg, of our fur department," said Una. "Now *I* was thinking of this . . ." she picked up one, and held it ready to put on. Ann slipped her arms into a softness, a featherweight caress, and regarded the mirror. If the suit had made her a young peeress, the coat elevated her to a young princess, regally framed and magnified by the thick silver-grey of Australian opposum. She began smiling all over her face, like a fool, then glanced half-apologetically at the two girls; their responsive smiles buttressed her and cheered her on.

"Will you try on some of these other coats?" invited Una.

"After this?" countered Ann, almost belligerently, and with a gesture cast the heap of glossy browns and blacks into outer darkness. "I should say not."

Una, beaming, lifted her book. "It's a charge, isn't it?"

The formalities dispatched, Ann said, "Could I wear these things out?" For she found herself strangely unable to sustain the most temporary of separations from the blue suit.

"Certainly," said Una. "I'll send your old ones."

"And on what floor —" she was getting rigged-out like a brass monkey, she thought, and why not? "— on what floor is the hairdresser?"

"Fifth," said Una. "Listen, ask for Mr. Carl."

Some two hours later she marched, with a conquering step, toward the lot where she had parked her car. On the thick russet-brown cap — very striking and arresting — that Mr. Carl had made of the hair, perched a sort of crushed blue cone, an Italian import, wonderfully crazy and becoming. People looked at her as she passed with her chin up and her mouth sweet with an involuntary smile; she walked along on air, borne up by a vast, indefinite happiness. This feeling of power and confidence companioned her increasingly all the way home. She had had enough of being timid and mealy-mouthed with that man; she would be poised and full of certainty from now on, able to control and shape events to her own desire. Out of mere exuberance she took the sharp left-hand turn into the driveway much too fast, and shot into the garage; then entered the house by the rear hall door.

Hardly was she in her own room when the bell rang; a moment later, Bessie was admitting someone.

On the instant — before he said good-day to Bessie, even — she knew in every fibre of her body who it was. Could it have happened more wonderfully? Just when she was polished to her uttermost gloss, more attractive than ever before in her life . . . she could have hugged herself for joy, only she was too busy calculating. First he would take off his topcoat, then go upstairs to Myra. When he came down again, and was putting on his coat — that was her chance; that half-minute or so. She would saunter out of course by accident, and let him have the full impact of the new hairdo and the new blue suit. She felt tall, triumphant, the conqueror, in advance, of anyone in the world — except that in all the world there was only one person that she wanted to conquer.

She settled down to wait for the sound of his descending footsteps. Meanwhile she anxiously burnished her hairdo, again and again, with the palm of her hand. And she still felt that lofty certainty — of course — but her breathing was strangely erratic, and she had difficulty in swallowing.

Connie, driving up Myra's street, decided to

park in front of the house, rather than go up the driveway to the turn-around; instinctively, by this act of a stranger, dissociating herself from the family, once and for all. Beneath her apparent composure she was grimly intent, if somewhat shaky, about the approaching encounter. She had rehearsed her attack at every point – as much as was possible – and stood braced to meet Myra's every recognition of the weaknesses of her position. Yes, it should be all right. Much would depend – of course – on the way she carried it off.

Arriving, she parked – on a sudden calculation – two houses below Myra's, rather than in view of her mother-in-law's bedroom windows; she was giving the victim no chance to see her and send Bessie down with a message that she was too ill for visitors. Softly she fitted her key into the door, turned it. (How convenient that Bruce's key had completely escaped Myra's memory.) The door opened quietly, and she stepped into the hall.

A man was coming down the stairs.

Connie halted in her tracks; the man halted too; their eyes met, held. Then he completed his descent, much more slowly; their eyes never moved apart. Her image, though it had somewhat faded from his horizon, had by no means disappeared, and now – here she was.

In Connie had revived, on the instant of seeing him again, that same inward shock of excitement as the first time. Intervening events had pushed him from her mind somewhat, it was true (besides, she was sleeping on and off with Gil Hubbard) but his actual presence brought back all the clamor and ravagement of desire, as before. The hell with Myra, she reflected, Myra could wait; Myra would be there tomorrow. He was here today — it was all that mattered.

In the half-dark, a strange thing happened. Without a word, with a queer precognition, a mindless animal compulsion, they moved together. Without touching each other otherwise, their lips fastened and locked, and for a blind interval exchanged such satisfactory assurances of experience as to force a soft groan from him, there in the dusky hall. When they separated, Connie was as badly off; her eyes were empty and her legs like straw, so that she could hardly stand. They were silent a few moments, still staring at each other in a sort of hypnosis. Then,

"Where are you going now?" she breathed.

"Nowhere." His voice, like hers, was barely audible; they stood in the hall like a couple of conspirators. "It's Saturday — no office hours."

"My place," she said peremptorily. "We'll go to my place."

"I haven't my car," he said. "It's at the shop."

"I've mine," she answered. "I'll drive you back – or wherever you want to go – later."

As they moved toward the door, "Be careful," she muttered. He nodded. Then they were outside, and his hand released the knob without a sound.

There, there, thought Ann, shamelessly on guard at her closed door: now he was coming downstairs. Her alertness, excitement and delicious fear redoubled. He remained in the hall so very briefly after his descent; her emergence, to seem casual, must be a matter of split-second timing. But she was expert in listening to, and interpreting, the sound of his movements. Then – surprisingly – came the curiously soft sound of the outside door opening and shutting. Had someone come in? Frowning, she listened. Or could he have left, at that improbable rate of speed, without the least pause for putting on his coat? It was a cold day; besides, by the sound, he had not even gotten all the way downstairs. She listened again. No sound – of voices or movement – no sound of any kind. But it was queer; in the silence out there she had a perception of presences, of something going on.

With the utmost, painful precaution, she eased open her door the least trifle.

Then she looked out, into the hall.

CHAPTER 18

"You're a good driver," he said, with involuntary admiration; they were going like the wind.

"I drove for some phony general during the War," she answered. Her voice, clear but curiously toneless, fell on his ear ungratefully, though this feeling, almost unconscious, was obscured by more prominent reactions. "Not a real general, a desk general," she was going on, and added casually, "I'm not a bad mechanic, either. What's wrong with your car?"

"Starter," he answered. "It stalls — mostly when I'm in a hurry, of course."

"Of course," she agreed. For a fraction of a second she looked full at him, then back to the road, and he felt a perceptible — and not pleasant — shock. In the dimness of the hall he had taken her eyes for light grey or blue; now, in the brilliant sunlight, and for the first time, he saw their actual color. Saw, but could not define, for the first comparison that occurred to him — of an albino's eyes — was manifestly not the right one. Yet they were grey, in a sense . . . lead-colored? no. Then he had it. They were silvery — a cold silver-grey or greyish-silver, not unlike frosted glass; the effect was doubly strange because her eyes were large. The pupils, contracted by the intense sunshine to dots, were most disconcerting of all; two black, intense dots in the middle of that cold, empty silver. The effect, somehow, was not exactly human. One terror of his infancy had been an illustrated version of the Spider and the Fly, and her eyes made him think of the pictured Spider's. As this occurred to him he exclaimed suddenly, "For God's sake!" The car swerved violently, just avoiding a cat whose dash across the road had been a miracle of bad timing.

"You almost hit that," he said, and she murmured, "Oh no." For a moment, still queasy over the cat's hairbreadth escape, he thought but was not sure that she smiled peculiarly — secretively? . . . They were doing over sixty, tearing past a district that was still farmland; she was concentrated on the road, and he was able to observe her, uninterruptedly if inconspicuously. There was something about her posture as she drove . . . she was hunched-over, almost, as if in pain or at least discomfort. He was actually about to inquire, when the truth dawned on him; she was crouched, not hunched – crouched like an animal about to spring. An unexpected distaste was spreading through him, and he remembered, suddenly, the aftermath of his first encounter with her. The fleeting chill, that undefined aversion ... but his subconscious had defined it then, and his conscious did now – with the former several jumps ahead, as usual. He glanced at her again, and this time she seemed to him less a woman than a bundle of naked instincts. And it was this very nakedness in her that repelled, almost intimidated him; a nakedness hungry, indecent, communicated from herself to the mad pace of the car. The current that had driven him toward her was carrying him away from her, and with equal speed; a revulsion had set in, more powerful than the perverse attraction. Again he thought of those pale eyes, and into his mind, suddenly and completely, there leaped a vision. The synapta. That blind greed, those furred creeping fingers, avid ...

The car was slowing down – for a turn into some nearby lane, he realized with a sinking heart; they were arriving. It was out of the question, his going into the house with her now; in the sudden and violent aversion that he felt, he had gone as dead as mutton. Now there loomed the unpleasant problem of extricating himself from the situation. He squared himself to meet it, while his heart sank again; however he handled it, this was going to be bad.

The car turned at a swinging wooden sign, between neglected gateposts overgrown with withered vines, and stopped before a small house. She killed the engine, and in the moment of quiet they sat unmoving; once more she turned that inhuman, lunar gaze on him.

"My God." He said it with artificial dismay, as if smitten by recollection, and followed through with an equally artificial laugh. "My God."

"What?" she murmured. There was an instant drawing-back in her, a sudden watchfulness.

"I've a hospital appointment in a half-hour." Whether it sounded convincing or not, he had no idea. "It went clean out of my head. Your fault," he added, with sickly jocularity.

She continued to sit perfectly motionless; no feature of her face had moved. Yet she changed completely; a venom almost tangible seemed to distill from her. She flicked him with a look from under suddenly hooded lids, while a sort of spasm curled from her nostrils to the corners of her mouth. The effect was one of extraordinary cruelty, of malevolence, and of more — of profound corruptness. She had seen through him, of course; he must have done it even worse than he had feared.

"I'll have to go at once," he said. His sudden unease was at least equal to his embarrassment. For the next development, he was totally unprepared. One of her slender hands shot out and scraped nail-marks across his face.

"Get out," said Connie.

He sat stupefied.

"Get out of my car," she repeated, following up this injunction with a few words that startled even him. His power of motion returned; he climbed out. "Walk back," she almost whispered. "Have a nice walk."

She remained sitting in the car, not even turning her head to follow his progress between the gateposts.

Ann lay exactly where she had fallen on the bed, years ago. Then the afternoon sun had been bright outside; now it was completely dark, the early dark of Winter evenings. There was something unnatural about her stillness, but her mind was not still; it ran in tormented circles, seeking escape from the nightmare in the hall. But there was no escape. If she opened her eyes, she saw them; if she closed her eyes, she still saw them. They had been as motionless as two statues; her head lifted, his bent; their lips holding together with that horrible force, though curiously she had no memory of any embrace of arms . . . but what she remembered was enough. She was still in the abyss, in the clammy aftermath of that first devastating cold sweat; she felt chilled to the bone, deathly sick. *How long can a person stand this?* she thought, for the hundredth time. Feebly, in her mind, she tried to run away, to burrow into some deeper dark and lie there, mindless. . . .

A sound impinged upon her death, dimly, then more distinctly; a knock at the door. *Go away, go away,* her mind prayed, *I can't. Who-ever it is, I can't.*

The knock was repeated; then the door opened a trifle, cautiously.

"Miss Ann?" It was Bessie. "Dinner in —" she broke off. "Why're you lying in the dark? don't you feel well?"

"Oh, hello, Bessie," It was her own voice, incredibly, quite ordinary-sounding and natural, perhaps slightly muffled. "No, I don't feel too well. I think I'm getting a cold."

"You kind of sound that way," said Bessie. "Well, dinner in ten minutes. You eat some hot dinner, it'll do you good."

"Oh, I couldn't, Bessie," said Ann. A giant qualm turned her inside-out. "I couldn't."

"Not just a little?" Bessie persisted. "I've got lovely creamed chicken and sweet-potato puff and a good rich pudding with hard sauce. Come on, Miss Ann, try, just a little."

"I couldn't," she gasped. In a moment she would scream or yell or be violently sick, right before Bessie. "I just want to sleep."

There was a moment of silence, then a restful grunt. "H'm!" said Bessie. "And your mother just wanting a small tray in her room. Fix a good dinner, then nobody eats it." The door closed with a slight thud, and the agonizing deliverance of being alone again was almost ecstasy, almost a joy. Then, for the first time, she realized that she had lain down in the new blue suit — a witness, like herself, of the episode in the hall.

"I can't wear that thing again," she thought wildly. "I'll burn it up."

Another thought seared her. "My, but I was going to mow him down," she thought, with flagellating self-mockery. "I was just going to bowl him over."

She rolled over, burying her face in the pillow, and began shaking with laughter.

CHAPTER 19

The weather broke suddenly; Sunday was bleak, sleeting and raining by turns, with an inimical wind straight from the East. Overnight the rain dried off, but the temperature fell another ten degrees; Monday was a day of cloudy cold, of still, leaden light.

By this light Ann, in the living-room at the moment, saw the wan shadow diagonally cast — the shadow of someone at the front door. By a sixth sense she knew whom; by some other instinct, too lightning-like for thought or calculation, she was making for the backstairs, a short flight that ran up from the pantry. Before dashing up she heard the voices in the kitchen — of Myra, who had made one of her very infrequent descents from her room some minutes before, and of Bessie.

On the second floor she entered the bedroom, and without an instant's hesitation took cover in the clothes-closet. It was enormous, wide and deep, with every gadget and frill ever invented for closets; from a pole at the rear hung a solid row of long plastic containers through which appeared, in dim Neapolitan layers, the pastels of Myra's evening dresses and coats. Shoving between the soft, swinging bulk of two of them, she found plenty of space in which to stand. Behind this barricade she was perfectly invisible; she had left the door open the merest crack, and it was improbable that anyone would notice the closet at just this juncture.

So far, the quickness of her action had outpaced emotion of any sort. But now vacillation and dread caught up with her, and other formless terrors beside. Her heart started to beat with heavy, sickening thuds, and a responsive big pulse hammered in her throat and cut off her breath.

Then, in the hall, she heard the footsteps of the two who were approaching the room in silence — Myra, and the other woman behind her.

Myra pushed the door shut and faced Connie.

"I told you to stay away from me." Her voice was stretched tight and thin, a rusty wire of pure hatred.

"Let's sit down," said Connie.

"No, let's not sit down."

"All right, let's do it on our feet."

"I know what you want —" Myra began.

"No, you don't," Connie interrupted her.

"I know exactly what you want, and the answer is no — it's NO, do you hear? I knew you'd try this again — though I didn't think even you would have the gall, so soon. I'll see you in hell before I give you another cent, do you understand?"

"You needn't scream, I can hear you," said Connie composedly, "and you're talking through your hat, of course — so long as I've got that diary."

"Diary!" Myra's laugh was shrill and spiteful. "Diary! stuff your diary. I was a fool that first time, my *God* was I a fool, just shelling out like that —" she had to stop for breath, "— but not again, my lovely little blackmailer, you've seen the last cent out of me. You took me by surprise that first time, but now I've had time to think. I'll — bet — anything —" she ground out each word "— I'll bet anything there's not a thing in that diary that anyone could make head or tail of — any stranger, I mean. You, you bloodsucker, you clamped onto a hint of some kind, that's all — but you can't make trouble for me with hints, especially not now, not twelve years later. Why, I'll bet —" Myra's voice was rocketing to the upper altitudes of challenge and defiance, before she snatched it back to a more cautious pitch "— I'll bet your whole story's phoney, all lies and bluff — you've been bluffing with nothing in your hand, or practically nothing. I'll bet my last nickel that's so!" she finished, her voice escaping again in a sort of yell. "I'll bet anything I've got!"

"Don't bet," said Connie. "You'd lose."

"Liar," said Myra. "You've nothing to back that up with. You'd never dare tell me what Archie wrote, because you know there's nothing. Go ahead, tell me what he wrote, I dare you —" Her voice thickened suddenly, failed; she swayed. Connie caught her elbow, lowered her to a chair, and said, "Where's that bottle? — Oh yes, I see it." It was near at hand, on a table. She uncapped it, handed the rod to Myra, and waited composedly for a long two or three minutes. Myra sat perfectly still; she breathed badly, and the chalky pallor of her face was enlivened, around the lips, with a pale blue ring. Even when she had obviously begun recovering, she continued to sit with her eyes closed, as if dreading to open them.

"Well now, you see," said Connie reasonably. "It's not a good idea, kicking up all this row. I can stand it perfectly well, but you can't."

Myra sat as before, in the protective darkness of her closed eyes, with no sign that she had heard.

"You were daring me to tell you what Archie wrote," Connie pursued. Her follow-through of this touchy subject might prove disastrous, it was true, but it had to be done. "Do you still dare me?"

Myra opened her eyes. "Yes," she said, looking at her daughter-in-law implacably. "Yes."

Connie steeled herself momentarily, before taking the first, irrevocable step onto that ground whose scanty footholds of fact were dotted, so sparsely and so far apart, among the quicksands of conjecture.

"All right," said Connie, with daunting crispness and positiveness. "Well, you thought up this idea. Then you got all three of them to come in with you — Luanna, Archie and Theo. You planned it — so that each of them had one particular thing to do. Then, you went to the old lady's house one day. You got the nurse to go for a drive with Theo and Luanna. That was Theo's part — keeping the nurse out of the way while you attended to the old girl. And you'd picked the maid's day off, with just the cook down in the kitchen, and she wouldn't be likely to come upstairs. Then you posted

Archie in front of the old lady's door while you went in and did the job. That was Archie's part – to warn you if anyone came. And your part –" she stopped short; there was a moment's complete silence.

"Yes?" challenged Myra. She could be seen to take instant heart at Connie's pause, and waited, wary and intent, with slitted eyes; with the beginnings, almost, of a smile.

"Your part's later," Connie said softly. "Before your part, came . . . Luanna's part." It was so largely guess-work from here on that she was cold with misgiving as she continued – noting, however, that the mention of Luanna had wiped the half-smile off Myra's face with gratifying abruptness.

"Luanna's part," she repeated, "was to steal a hypodermic from that Dr. Peters. And she did it." Bull's-eye, Connie thought deliriously, she had scored; the stricken look on Myra's face told her so.

"But Luanna was a softie," she went on, "a weak sister. She's the one you'd expect to go all to pieces, and she did. It was on her conscience, she had to talk about it. So she talked to Archie. And Archie put it all down – in his little green book."

On a sudden flash of inspiration, she began to improvise, a delirious feeling of ascendancy, stronger than reason, assured her she would get away with it.

"Luanna saw you doing some awfully funny things with that needle," she lied fluently, out of whole cloth. "It worried her to death, and of course she had to spill it to Archie —"

"All right!" Myra cried out in an appalling voice. "All right, all right." Her face was damp and ashen, an old, hollow mask of despair, with dark pits for eyes and a tight-clamped mouth; she was fighting to breathe as if in a vacuum. Connie observed these manifestations with bright-eyed, detached interest, while congratulating herself inwardly. That was luck, to have her narrative cut off before it reached the one detail she could not supply — the contents of the lethal hypodermic; that was real luck.

"How much?" It was not Myra's voice, but its ghost. "How much — this time?"

Connie paused only minutely.

"A hundred thousand dollars," she said, in a gentle voice.

"A hundred . . ." In the pent-up silence, Myra seemed to be winding up like a spring, tighter, tighter . . . the silence exploded.

"No!" she screeched, with all her lungs. "No!" She burst into strangling sobs; she hammered the chair-arms with her clenched fists, then gripped her head in both hands as if to keep it from flying apart, then hammered again. "No!" she kept wailing. "No, no, no, no!"

"Look," said Connie reasonably, talking against the din; Myra was apparently ready to keep it up for a long time. "Look, be sensible about this," she went on in a raised voice. "Why's it so bad, after all?"

"Why's it so bad!" Myra echoed, frantically. "It's almost half of all I've got, *half*, damn you —"

"But I'm leaving you half," Connie interrupted. "After all, how long do you expect to live? Ten years, say at the outside? That means you've ten thousand a year for the rest of your life, and pretty good, too. I'm being more generous to you than you were to me."

"You're being generous to me — on my own money — thanks!" Myra uttered a wild laugh. "I can start wrecking my capital, can I? the only security I've got?"

"Why not?" shrugged Connie. "Archie got along all right on his capital. Of course he ran through most of it," she soliloquized maliciously, "but he died before it all went up the flue. You might not time it that well — you might go on living after your money's gone. But *I* don't think you'll last that long."

Again Myra started weeping; on a new note,

beaten and hopeless. "Aren't you ashamed?" she blubbered. "Aren't you ashamed?"

"Ashamed?" smiled Connie. "What of? Are you ashamed of what you did to that old woman?"

Myra rallied suddenly. "I – won't – give – you – a – cent!" She flung the words, like so many separate pellets, into Connie's face. But it was plainly a last stand; her emphasis was too frantic to carry conviction. "I won't give you a penny!" Her exhausted voice spun up to a shout, cracked. "I'll see you in hell first, and do what you like. Show the book to the police – do anything you want, you leech, you bloodsucker – run to the police. They *can't* do anything, it was too long ago. Do what you like, and be damned to you!" Her final shriek left an emptiness in the air, a hiatus. Into this, after a moment, gently fell Connie's voice.

"It isn't just a question of my taking the diary to the police," she said in a pleasant voice. "The diary isn't all you have to worry about – not by a long shot." She paused a moment, enjoying Myra's look of renewed apprehension. "Archie's dead, Luanna's nuts. But Theo . . ." She let another slight pause intervene. "Theo's alive. If I put them onto him, and they asked him a few questions . . . well, you know him." She smiled. "I'd hate *my* safety to depend on Theo's keeping his mouth shut. I can just see him coming unstuck right away — like a wet paper bag. He's like Luanna that way — sort of a weak link." She smiled again. "And it was a long time ago, yes, but I understand they never close the book on murder, there's no statute of limitations — on murder." Myra, she observed, had gotten still paler; it had not seemed possible, but she had done it.

"Of course I don't expect you to get a hundred thousand in a couple of days, like last time," she continued affably. "I'll give you a month, even six weeks. I'll be perfectly reasonable, if —" she stressed the last word delicately "— if you'll be reasonable."

Myra began to cry again; an ululation from the depths, a long-drawn-out lamentation.

"If you'd been decent to me when I was absolutely strapped and up against it," said Connie, "none of this would have happened. I'd have remembered to give you the diary and that would have been that. Still, this way's better for me, in the end, isn't it? Your own meanness brought this on you — and serve you right."

Myra's sustained cadences of grief broke off abruptly. "Monster!" she screamed. "You monster!"

"No worse monster than you," answered

Connie placidly. "And I don't smile all the time, at least. – I won't come around again, but I'll phone," she concluded. "Remember, in a month to six weeks. That's lots of time to raise the cash."

She left the house walking on air; she had brought it off. That sudden, dangerous guess back there – about Luanna's seeing Myra with the hypodermic – had been very precarious; if she had been wrong, the whole show must necessarily have been given away. But she had not been wrong; she had been on the ball from the first. *You're a good guesser, honey,* she told herself smugly. Then she slammed the convertible's door and took the car away from the curb in a long, beautiful, victorious swoop.

Ann, hardly breathing, eased herself out of the closet. If Myra, prostrate on the bed, should open her eyes at just this moment, and see her . . . but the spent figure lying there never moved; there was no more motion to it than to a waxwork. She got clear of the closet and with infinite caution inched a few steps toward the bedroom door . . . Myra opened her eyes and looked straight at her. The blackness of panic commenced swimming up into her head – until she saw that Myra had no idea she had entered in any but the usual way, for she only said in a ravaged voice, "What do you want?"

"I just got home," Ann stammered, recovering quickly. "I thought you called me."

Myra shook her head slightly, a scarcely-accomplished motion out of some depth of utter depletion; she looked blanched, blotted-out.

"I want to sleep," she muttered. Then she turned her head to the wall and again lay motionless.

CHAPTER 20

Ann only paused in the hall to snatch up a coat, then closed the front door noiselessly behind her and ran up the driveway to the garage. As she flung herself into her car, obeying the almost crazy need for action that drove her along with no volition of her own, she was mindless but for one thought: the diary, Archie's diary, that Connie was holding over Myra's head. But Connie was improvident, a sloven; although she might hardly carry it about on her person, it was equally unlikely that she would have rented a lockbox, say, to put it in. So the liveliest probability was that she merely kept it at home, well or poorly hidden. As for this hiding-place . . .

"I should be able to think up anything *she* can think up," Ann reflected scornfully. She had long had a comprehensive and rather priggish contempt for Connie's intellectual ability.

The car was cold; she gunned it ruthlessly,

her foot striking and stamping down on the starter. Then she backed into the street with reckless speed, righted the car, and started driving fast. Of a plan, she had not the least vestige; an urgency outside of herself was moving her.

However, when she had gone a few miles, there began returning to her mind, in some small measure, the faculty of planning. She had never been in Connie's house, but she knew where it was; that is, she had driven past the kennels many times, and knew that Connie rented a small house on the property. All depended, now, on whether she had gone straight home after the blackmailing interview with Myra. Ann rather thought not, knowing her sister-in-law's restless horror of staying at home alone; death rather. Still, if Connie *were* at home now ... then she must make the attempt tomorrow, or on the next day; she would hang around the place, keeping out of sight as best she could, until she saw Connie leave; she would keep trying and trying until she got into that house. . . .

Here it was; at least, here was the swinging wooden sign of the kennels, and the little house just past the gate must be it. On impulse she drove the car fifty feet further along, turned into the road-verge as close among the trees as she could get, and went back on foot. Connie was out; this discovery half-pleased, half-frightened her. No concealing that loud convertible, and there was no garage nearby where she could put it — at least none that Ann could see.

The gatehouse's front door had a good solid look; its upper third consisted of a glass panel through which she peered into an unlighted living-room, empty. For precaution's sake she knocked loudly a couple of times, aware that her last vestige of fear had been driven out by her obsessing sense of what she must do. Only silence responded to her thumpings; the house looked empty and sounded empty. She tried the door, which was locked — of course. Quickly she went around to the back. Yes, there was a back door, a much-less-solid affair than the front one; this was also locked, but it shook to and fro in a weak, rattletrap way as she tried it. Drawing off, she threw her full weight against it. It gave perceptibly, but still the lock held. Raising her foot — in a stout walking shoe — she kicked hard at the lock. On her second try there was a snapping sound, and the door flew open.

She stepped inside, closing it behind her. She was in a minute kitchen, whose sink, drainboard and table were full of dirty dishes.

A sudden loud rustling made her heart stand still, until she realized; mice, of course. Here, there and everywhere stood remnants of food and overflowing ashtrays; bloated butts drowned in the dregs of coffee, or lay sodden and obscene upon saucers. Somehow she felt that the kitchen was not the hiding-place — and yet it might be, anything might be. For that matter, what if Connie carried it around with her? There were too many possibilities; her heart sank.

The living-room was very small, sparsely and shabbily furnished, and its fireplace, degraded to the function of a catch-all, contained a huge rat's nest of trash. A short flight of steps ascended along one wall, so there must be an upstairs bedroom. Dismay chilled her again; even in a small house, there were scores of probable hiding-places ... well, for better or worse, she must begin somewhere. At least there was not much furniture and no drapes, no books, and hardly any magazines.

She began opening drawers, thrusting her hand under cushions, under the couchcover, finally moving the couch itself away from the wall; she turned a couple of pottery jars upside-down, felt behind all the pictures on the wall. Nothing whatever. Throwing a final hopeless glance about, she went hastily upstairs. The bedroom, disheveled, presented a messier problem. She investigated the tumbled bed, took all the drawers out of the chest, picked up the rugs, canvassed the small closet; after this she went into the bathroom, and with a growing sense of futility opened the medicine closet, then dumped the contents of the hamper on the floor, felt them over, and dumped them back again. On a stray recollection from many detective-stories, she even lifted the lid of the tank, a repository for hidden articles in the best tradition. Nothing. She went downstairs again. Standing perfectly still, she contemplated the living-room. For no reason, during the next few minutes, her eyes returned again and again to the naked fireplace. This, like so many of its ilk in the country, had obviously been sealed up at one time, and a stove placed in front of it; in later years it had been opened once more. But a vestige of the stove still remained in its opening for the pipe, centrally pierced in the chimney-breast, near the low ceiling; over it had been placed the customary tin cap with fluted edges and cardboard center, this one bearing a faded winter-scene.

She walked to the fireplace and peered upward. The cap, when she stood directly under it, seemed insecure, as if hanging on loosely. She reached up and took hold of the rim, which lifted off at once without resistance, disclosing the gaping mouth of the old tin pipe. Into this she reached her hand; instantly her fingers encountered the feel of leather, the shape of a small oblong. It had not been so hard after all. She had it, *she had it,* she thought wildly, holding the small book whose green-and-gold was sooty and smutty from the pipe in which it had lain.

Then, with a start, she saw that the light had faded considerably; that, engrossed in her search, she had lost all count of passing time; already she had been here much longer than she intended. Suddenly she was weak with nervousness. This bare, shabby little house, so still and silent; in the oncoming darkness it seemed, all at once, sinister . . . she must get out of here. She had taken one step toward the kitchen when some obscure compulsion, some sixth sense, made her glance toward the door. Through the glass panel appeared in silhouette a motionless head and shoulders, someone looking in at her . . . Connie.

Standing blankly in a vacuum of absolute terror, she heard, as from a distance, a key in the lock; then Connie was in the room. After that it was a nightmare jumble, a whirling pin-wheel of motion like a trick film. Connie darted at once to the fireplace, picked up the poker, and came straight at her. In the dusky room Ann was aware only of her eyes, those *white eyes* she had always called them to herself, coming nearer and nearer. . . . Without thought but with equal speed, she swung up a small chair and drove it, legs first, at Connie, who staggered backward in a sort of run and fell against the far wall. The worst of the poker's force had been deflected by the chair, but the sweep of Connie's arm had given it direction; it flew from her hand but kept on going, caroming off the corner of her eye and the point of her left cheekbone. A blinding pain split her head; she tottered and almost fell. Connie was already getting to her feet, and Ann veered drunkenly through the open door. Struggling along at a crippled run, with the rending pain in her head and eye confusing her sense of direction, she managed to scrabble past the gateposts and into the road. Here she started walking the wrong way for her car, then reversed herself and started back, all the while listening for Connie's footsteps behind her. But no one appeared, surprisingly; she felt a swimmy wonderment that Connie had abandoned the pursuit. Feebly she climbed into her car and sat, waiting for the pain and overpowering giddiness to subside. It was the darker end of twilight; not a soul was visible in the road. At last she started the car, driving slowly and cautiously, for the pain had resolved itself into a rhythmic stabbing and a bright pulsating cloud that stood continuously in front of her left eye. This loss of half her vision made it surprisingly hard to judge distances; things that seemed quite far away one moment were on top of her the next. Lucky that Connie had not pursued her outside and made a second attempt with the poker while she was in this rocky condition . . . a sudden realization, an icy shock, shattered her; tardily she understood why the pursuit had been abandoned. In snatching up the chair to parry the attack, she had dropped the diary. After all her effort, it was still Connie's, an instrument endowing her with the malevolent power of terrorizing, of extorting. . . .

Ann jerked the car to a stop with dangerous suddenness, and was violently sick in the road.

Ralph, letting himself out of the office very late, was closing the door at the same moment that he noted the parked car a little way down the street, and the woman getting out of it. She was doing it in the most precarious fashion, swaying outrageously; completely fried, of course. Then he realized that she was heading, or seemed to be heading, for the cement walk that led to his place. He hesitated; it was dark, there was no street lighting immediately nearby, and his not-very-sympathetic diagnosis of her condition was confirmed by her weaving, stumbling gait. And she had been driving a car, the damned fool, also it was no part of his professional activity to sober lushes. Now she was coming up the walk . . . another moment, and she would be on her face. He moved forward to help her. He had almost reached her, when suddenly she stopped dead for a moment, then fell on the ground at his feet.

Lying on the couch in the x-ray cubicle, she turned her head and looked at him, still only half-aware, but getting her bearings. Ralph, sitting beside the couch, met her look reassuringly. It had taken some doing to get her up off the cement walk without assistance and carry her in; she had been completely unconscious then.

"How did you get this?" he asked. "This" was a wicked-looking bruise that completely covered the left upper cheek and left temple. Whatever it was, she had narrowly escaped having the cheekbone smashed and the left eye damaged, even destroyed. Luckily the x-ray showed nothing in the way of fracture, only severe contusions; even so, she could hardly feel disposed for conversation. But she was no longer dazed, for her eyes met his intelligently; she could answer one or two questions. "How did it happen?" he repeated.

"I – I skidded," she answered laboriously, in a lifeless voice.

"Skidded?"

"Yes," she said, adding after a moment, "I hit my face against the wheel."

"There's been no rain," he pointed out. "Why should you skid?"

"I don't know why," she answered, still in that dead, laborious tone. "It just happened."

"In that case –" he was considering, frowning, "– I should think the front of your face would have taken the beating – chiefly the nose, and maybe a bad wallop on your upper teeth."

She concentrated on this – with an effort, it seemed, and replied, "I was thrown against the door."

"You just said you hit yourself on the wheel."

"Did I?" She still seemed cloudy, but he felt her suddenly heightened access of wariness – of calculation. "I guess I made a mistake. Yes, I distinctly remember it was the door." She closed her eyes again.

For some moments he considered her sceptically, in silence. The nature of the bruises, and her account of them, were completely at variance; the flat surface of unbroken glass could never produce those particular marks, above all at two such unrelated angles. Better, though, not to hound her for the truth at present; she was far from up to it, he decided, as she opened her eyes and looked at him again.

At this moment, and for the first time, something else dawned upon him. He had been so engrossed with examining the injury itself, with the x-ray and so forth, that another aspect of her appearance had escaped him. But now he saw that she lay in a stony quiet, an unnatural remoteness. It reminded him of the way people looked after a . . . after a death, that was it. Yes, that was exactly her appearance – stricken, wrapped in that strange otherwhereness – and from it she looked out indifferently, uncaringly. His mother, after his father's death, had looked at him in that same way, from that same incalculable distance, as if hardly seeing him or knowing him. Grieving people had no eyes for you; they could only contemplate, in some aghast, unbelieving trance, their own grief. But he doubted that her accident alone could account for that look. What the devil had happened to her?

By instinct alone, not logic, he began connecting the phenomenon in front of him with Connie; his contact with her had left him profoundly convinced that she was capable of anything. But he hesitated to ask. Difficult, to frame such an inquiry; almost impossible, in the face of this girl's patent attempt to mislead him.

Still, as a preliminary to some cautious tentative questioning, he picked up her hand with a soothing professional gesture. At once she shrank from him; hardly with any external movement of her body, but with a deep and inward shrinking. Astounded, he released the hand, staring at her. His astonishment, short-lived, was succeeded by a sudden unpleasant certainty, incontrovertible. All right, she had seen him in the hall with Connie. And what of it? it was none of her God-damned business — he was under no obligation to account to her. But in the same instant he discovered in himself, not only too much defiance, but an astounding regret; the extent of his unwillingness to have had her see it amazed him. Well, with this wall suddenly risen between them, he would have to give up — for the present — his project of questioning her; and he felt that this postponement, for some indefinable reason, might have bad consequences. Well, there was no help for it; it was all very unfortunate. Their eyes, caught in a stare, released each other in the same embarrassed moment, and he said with detachment, "I'll drive you home."

"I can drive," She supported her assertion by raising up, and had to fall back.

"You can drive in a week, if that," he said coldly. "A head-injury's always precarious. You don't want to go blacking-out and piling up against a telephone-pole, do you? No driving until I say, understand?"

"I understand," she said with equal coldness. He helped her up off the couch, touching her as little as possible, since contact with him seemed unendurable to her, and with the same fingertip aloofness helped her on with her coat, out of the building, and into his car. He drove fast, in perfect silence, always aware of the profile that never turned toward him. Not pretty, that profile, but so individual that it had almost a beauty of its own; she possessed a degree of personality striking in so young a girl. These considerations faded in his renewed awareness of her aura of despair; this was so strong that he could hardly believe it derived from the situation between themselves — it was something far more serious. What disaster could have befallen her to account for that crushed aspect, that look of hopeless, averted grief?

They arrived; he helped her out, unlocked the door for her and said goodnight briefly, adding, "I'll have your car driven around tomorrow."

She nodded; the hall light struck downward on the cruel bruise with its implications of some violent, hidden episode ... like a thunderclap there struck him the thought of rape, staggering. For a moment he felt a tumultous need to question her, get the truth out of her; her depleted look forbade him. Then he felt a need, almost as imperious, to hold her close in his arms, protectively; again her sealed face and withdrawn eyes, by no conscious effort of her own, imposed a total barrier.

"I'll want to look at this again," he said, indicating the bruise, and left her.

Going down the walk, he was still unpleasantly disturbed by his shocking idea, and to throw it off reflected that his conclusion had probably been absurdly farfetched. But she would have a fine black eye tomorrow, poor child. Then he thought of this further outrage upon her creamy skin, and cursed his moment of semi-amusement. Also, she had certainly seen him in the hall with Connie; he was positive of it now. A fine tableau they must have presented, he and she . . . treading down violently on the starter, he struck his foot at a bad angle, and the moment of acute pain somehow made him feel better.

CHAPTER 21

Connie stood in the night-darkened driveway, staring at the windows of Ann's room. These were uncurtained, and even this late the blinds were not lowered. The room appeared dimly lighted – mostly by firelight, apparently – and from time to time Ann moved into range of the windows. At these times Connie's gaze took on a bird-of-prey fixity, while her face contracted with a sort of hunger and the extreme tip of her tongue came out and just barely touched her lips. Her original but inactive dislike of her sister-in-law had flared up, through the events of the last few days, into a cold, still hatred; an exterminating hatred with its roots in the very marrow of her bones. It was cold out here in the driveway, but the cold and dark of the wintry night accorded well with something inhuman inside of her; she smiled momentarily, thinking of Ann in there and herself out here, and how Ann would feel if she knew herself the object of this secret watch from the night shadows.

Nor was it for the mere indulging of malevolence that Connie had come here every evening for the last week or so, but for the exercise of a tangible plan – prevented from developing, however, by the (unconscious) interference of Bessie. The big garage doors were invariably kept locked – for this Connie had been prepared – but now the side door into the garage was locked as well, all the time. This was a complete departure from custom, but Bessie had figured that while her employer was seedy and using her car little or not at all, this extra precaution could do no harm. In the hope of finding the side door open at some time, Connie had regularly and nocturnally prowled her mother-in-law's property – with, so far, no success. But curiously enough, this did not irk her. She felt within herself a secret power, an inexhaustible patience; a voluptuousness, almost, of waiting. There was no hurry; she had all the time in the world. Sooner or later the opportunity would come.

Now, before leaving, she started on a final noiseless patrol toward the rear of the house. It was perfectly safe; the kitchen had been dark for some time. But as she followed the side of the house around the corner, something peculiar happened. Peculiar enough, at least, to make her pull up short, puzzled.

A blast of heat seemed to come at her, improbably, from the wall of the house itself – from that section of wall along which she was passing. She laid her hand on it, and had to snatch it back; even with her gloves on, the stucco surface was too hot for endurance. With sudden interest she concentrated on this phenomenon, which surely was not normal. Then the explanation dawned on her, or at least she believed so. She longed to turn her flashlight on the wall and examine it, but dared not risk any action that might betray her presence in this place; everything depended on her remaining unseen.

Walking down the driveway, cat-footed, she decided that the end of the Winter afternoon was her best bet. She must time herself to get there just before dark; neither too early nor too late. After all, no great amount of light was needed for examining the wall of a house. And – if the manifestation turned out to be what she supposed – she might as well avail herself of this opportunity so unexpectedly offered, as a supplement to her original plan. Of the two traps so painstakingly set, one or the other – given enough time – was sure to work.

Though she kept the fireplace blazing

continuously, piling on more and more logs and hunching as near it as possible, Ann always felt cold nowadays. The weight that rested on her was not to be lightened by so easy a means as tears, or similar discharge of emotional steam; no, this was trouble, real trouble, leaden and overshadowing, heavy and cold as the grave. The episode of the clothes-closet, the revelation of her mother's secret, the spectacle of her mother struggling in Connie's talons . . . that was the worst of the nightmare; Myra's utter helplessness, the fact that she could not invoke assistance against Connie without accusing herself. This horror almost eclipsed the other, somehow. Then her own failure to secure the diary – the key to the whole ugly affair – after actually having it in her hands; the thought of this drove her to the verge of frenzy.

Another desolation possessed her too, a pervasive, settled regret. She had been well aware for many years that there existed between Myra and herself no basis of true relationship or sympathy, that they cared for one another only in the automatic family sense; they might love, but did not like, each other. Now even this unsatisfactory bond had fallen away; and she felt, not liberation or relief, but a degree of pain that astonished herself, a sense of loss and impoverishment. As if she had lost someone by death, she thought; and she had lost her mother, and the loss of an unsatisfactory mother, even, apparently laid an axe of some sort to the roots of one's existence. In a moment of melancholy perception she surveyed the futility of uncongenial people fatally bound together for life by the indissoluble tie of blood; loving each other perhaps with an irritated love to their little benefit, or hating with a corrosive hatred to their infinite detriment.

Also, along with this sombre overcast − of oppression on her own account and dread on Myra's − went an acute recognition of her newly precarious situation. She must reckon herself with Connie's recently-stimulated enmity, knowing her sister-in-law far too well to suppose that this enmity would remain passive. But what form it would take was completely beyond her imagination, nor did she feel equal to much in the way of self-defense, at the moment. Gingerly she touched the fading bruises on her cheek and temple, which still ached. She could wait, that was all − wait and see what Connie would be up to. . . .

The footsteps in the hall, descending the stairs, had hardly penetrated her consciousness, but now came the knock at the door. She opened it; Ralph Markham stood there.

"May I speak to you a moment?" he said quickly, in a low, cautious voice. She stepped back; he came into the room, shutting the door behind them.

"I want you to know," he began without preamble, "that I don't like your mother's condition. I don't like it at all."

She waited, silent.

"She's taken another decisive turn for the worse, in this last week," he went on. "For instance, she's lost a lot of weight suddenly. That's never a good indication, least of all in a case like hers. She's losing ground, Miss Walworth," he pursued urgently. "More than I thought she'd lose in years. What's happened to bring this on, all of a sudden? You must know. What's happened to her recently?"

Why, nothing has happened to her, doctor. Except that my sister-in-law, the one you were kissing in the hall, has somehow gotten hold of a diary that belonged to my uncle. And this diary involves my mother in a murder; she and her sister and brothers got together and murdered their step-mother. So your girl-friend's using this diary to blackmail Mamma, and Mamma daren't do anything, don't you see? Because if she accuses Connie of blackmail, she accuses herself of murder. So she's been making a lot of trips to the bank in this terribly cold weather, when she shouldn't be out at all; I've followed her there in my car. She comes back from the bank and has one attack after another. No, nothing's happened to Mamma except blackmail, that's all. And it's eating her up, being trapped like that, she's wild with hatred and the feeling of being trapped, and it's killing her. Ask my sister-in-law about it, why don't you? the next time you're kissing her?

He waited for her reply, his eyes intent upon her. Aloud she said, economically, "Nothing special has happened to her recently." She was determined to hew to the bare line, to avoid at all costs any possibly-revealing embroidery.

"Look," he returned flatly, his eyes and voice hard with disbelief. "Something is driving her crazy. Unless it's lifted off her, I can't do a great deal. And you ask me to believe that you don't know anything about it?"

"She won't talk to me," she protested hurriedly. He was silent a moment, then said, "Well, if she won't be frank with me — and if you won't —" To the exasperation and finality in his voice she opposed a passive blankness; for some seconds they stood in a deadlock. Then he shrugged, started turning away, then turned again.

"Ann —" on impulse, he was hazarding an

inquiry doubtfully ethical, that in the ordinary course he would never dream of "— what about the idea you had before — that Mrs. Walworth had something to do with this condition of your mother's? Do you still think she's mixed up in it in any way?"

"Oh no," she answered promptly, in her alarm at the perilous question almost over-looking the heart-shaking fact that he had called her, for the first time, not Miss Walworth but *Ann*. "Mrs. Walworth has nothing to do with it." She could see his extreme surprise at her answer before he pointed out, "But at first you thought she had everything to do with it. You've certainly changed your mind."

"Yes, I have," she said briefly.

"You were sure though," he accused her. "You were so sure."

"I know. I was wrong." She continued doggedly, in the face of his evident disbelief. "They were just having an argument those two other times, that was all."

"How do you know?"

"My mother told me." She looked him composedly in the eye. "It was all my imagina-tion. Connie has nothing to do with this, nothing at all."

"Well —" he shrugged again; one corner of

his mouth twisted briefly, ironically. The little fool, with her first urgent accusation of Connie, and now her no less urgent retraction of that accusation; did she think she made sense with such irreconcilable extremes of conduct? And there was something disturbing in her tenacious — if transparent — lies, because lies and evasions were so at odds with her clear and simple personal quality.

Then there struck him, for the first time, another troubling implication of her appearance. The bruises on her face had faded out to an all-but-invisible mauve, but the face itself was shadowed and oppressed, an incongruous look in one so young; then that locked, impenetrable silence of hers. Also she was far too thin, and this change, too, had taken place in the last week or so.

"You don't look too flourishing yourself," he said. "Have you stopped eating?"

"Oh no." A shadowy smile barely woke in her face, was gone. "I eat like a horse."

"I can see that," he retorted, and with a feeling of helplessness took his departure. What in hell was going on in that house? he thought, driving away. That woman upstairs, with her rapid and mysterious deterioration plainly traceable to some inward rage that was tearing at her, so that the composite effect — of wild eyes, neglected hair and extreme thinness — was not far removed from mania; then the young one downstairs, with her haunted expression, her anxious, unconvincing lies, her look of sinking beneath some weight too heavy for her to bear ... what fantastic situation, what improbable circumstances, bound together these two hagridden creatures?

He suspected Connie, Ann thought; a fact, to her, completely incredible — his accusing a person with whom he was in love. And he was in love with Connie; she had seen it. Flinching momentarily from the unfading image of it, she reflected that she herself — irony of ironies — stood committed to the protection of Connie as if she were Ann's most cherished possession. Incredible, that she must throw a shield over the blackmailer, the extortioner — for any attempt to invoke outside assistance against Connie would result, inevitably, in Connie's retaliating upon Myra. She was caught and held, immobilized, between the prongs of the two opposing considerations; pinioned in a perpetual numbness, a standstill of despair.

In addition, she had in the past few days acquired a new habit — that of taking sleeping-pills. She had never done this in her life, but it was better than lying awake half the night, hearing Myra walk the floor at all hours of the night, and her occasional gusts of wild crying. The pills, mere advertised stuff sold over the counter, could hardly be very strong, but she seemed extremely susceptible to the sedative, whatever it was, for one of them knocked her out like a rabbit-punch. And an unpleasant feeling; it had nothing to do with real sleep. This was a suffocation, a saturating heaviness that pinned her down and would not let go. In this artificial sleep she would lie sodden for nine hours on end oblivious to ordinary sounds; once she had taken a pill, she had to sleep it out.

CHAPTER 22

Connie inserted the key noiselessly into the lock, and stepped inside the hall. Here she paused a moment, reconnoitring. Since Myra's car was in the garage, Myra herself was probably upstairs, well out of the way; and Ann's car had just driven away. For this, she had been watching and waiting. Bessie would be in the kitchen now, in the hour before dinnertime. She must work fast; she had not a moment to lose.

Passing silently through the hall and into Ann's room, she closed the door behind her as silently, and went directly to the fireplace. In this, a bed of embers still gave off considerable heat; not enough, though, to impede her examination. She picked up the poker, knelt down, probed gently between the bricks of the fireback. Yes, the mortar was crumbling at the point she touched — and here, and there; the whole fireback was riddled with cracks. She pushed a little harder, and with a slight crunching sound two or three more inches of poker vanished between the bricks. Under continuous high heat, the mortar of the fireback was wholly disintegrated. This was satisfactory, but there remained the chief question: was there wooden lath in that hot wall, or not? Probably it made no difference. The catti-corner fireplace and its chimney were contained in a section of masonry and stucco extending about four feet each way from the corner of the house; on either side and above this brief section, was clapboard.

Having pierced the fireback at a dozen points, she replaced the poker and went to the door, soft-footed. With the knob in her hand — and just on the point of turning it — she stopped dead. Someone was in the hall. . . .

The footsteps seemed moving toward this room; they hesitated, ceased; the person was standing there. Then, to Connie's relief, they went slowly toward the kitchen. Bessie, she conjectured, turning on the hall-light. She opened the door a crack; the soft illumination confirmed her guess. Quickly and noiselessly she left the room, let herself out, and went along the house to the outside wall of the fireplace. This, as she had surmised, proved to be cobwebbed with fine cracks, an unmistakable record of long-continued heat damage. Taking from her pocket a thin, narrow blade some ten inches long, which she had salvaged from the ruinous barn behind Lydia's workshop, she thrust it into one crack, then another. It failed to encounter wood — for this she had hardly hoped — but under pressure it penetrated, in some places, nearly its whole length. Rapidly she repeated the process at numerous points, casting watchful looks down the drive for Ann's return; it was almost dark now. But she finished without interruption, then walked swiftly to the street and regained her car, parked well around the corner.

Deep satisfaction filled her; it had been a good evening's work. The channels she had deepened and widened, inside and out, must meet in some places; it was only a question of waiting until enough heat got through to the wood beyond the stucco. And it was a marvelous idea, seeing that no sign of the tampering could possibly survive a fire. And if, by some fluke, no fire developed within a reasonable period, she could always fall back on her first idea, which centered, not in the house, but in the garage — and which was already put in train. It was only a question of which worked first; the outcome, in either case, should be the same.

Mr. Hulse and Mr. Landis exchanged glances of consternation and bafflement. On the older man's desk lay a large docket of lined and columned paper, with lists of holdings and investments; a representation, on paper, of Mrs. Walworth's pleasant little estate. At this Mr. Hulse glanced from time to time, and shook his head slightly.

"She must be nuts," Mr. Landis volunteered, after a silence.

Mr. Hulse said nothing.

"There's no other explanation," Mr. Landis added, after a further pause. "They say it's likely to happen with women of that age — go off their rocker all at once. Look at the way she's changed," he elaborated. "She looks crazy, if ever I saw anyone do."

"The whole thing's crazy," Mr. Hulse agreed. "The point is, what's her idea? — Of course," he mused, "you read stuff like that in the papers all the time — about some old pencil-woman or something, and they find her starved to death in an unheated room in the dead of Winter, and there's seventy or eighty thousand bucks in a hole in the wall or the teapot."

"Mrs. Walworth isn't any old pencil-woman," Mr. Landis pointed out, defending his erstwhile favorite.

"Maybe not," Mr. Hulse assented. "But over the past month she's turned into cash, and withdrawn —" he peered again at the docket with unbelieving eyes, though he knew the amount perfectly well, "— she's withdrawn and liquefied one hundred thousand dollars' worth of gilt-edged investments. That's virtually half the estate, within a few thousand. Why's she doing it?" he demanded again.

Mr. Landis was unhelpfully silent.

"And what's she doing *with* it?" reiterated Mr. Hulse.

CHAPTER 23

Myra came in out of the lethal January cold; as soon as she got through the door she stood still and began to cough, the deep, exhausting cough deriving from her complaint; she coughed and strangled and could not stop. When it abated, she began fighting for breath, harshly and audibly. Then she stood waiting for her strength to return, meanwhile eyeing the stairs with obvious dread, as if they were a sky-reaching obstacle. Finally beginning the ascent, she took it with immense slowness, bringing both feet to the same tread and stopping to rest three times on the single short flight. She disappeared upstairs at last; it had not seemed as though she would make it, but she had.

Ann turned away from the crack in the living-room door through which she had observed this performance — not less painful for having seen it two or three times before — with a sick heart and a destroying sense of impotence. She dared not go out and offer her help, having tried it before and been violently repulsed; Myra was almost dangerous to approach nowadays, perpetually in a state of something verging on frenzy. Ann knew, too, where Myra had been and what she had brought home with her. Always, before, when she returned from these excursions to the bank; when she labored her way up the steps and disappeared into her room, Ann had stood listening, listening; for what, she did not exactly know. And when nothing materialized, she always felt it a only a postponement, a short reprieve, in a progress toward some inevitable disaster. So now, in like manner, she stood listening; her head lifted toward the upstairs, her nerves tight with the cringing tightness of anticipation ... and at this moment the sound came, the heavy sound of a human body falling; the sound that, for the past few weeks, she had heard prophetically.

"Bessie!" she shouted, making for the stairs. "Bessie!" As she thudded up she heard the kitchen door flying open, and Bessie's rapid footsteps behind her.

"Thank you," said Ann.
"Nothing to thank me for," said Ralph, briefly.

Again they stood in the hall, which seemed curiously silent, like the whole house; especially in contrast to the clamor and flurry, an hour before, of Myra's collapse, the frantic telephoning, the doctor's rapid arrival followed by the ambulance, Myra's removal to the hospital, Ralph and Ann following in his car . . . all that had passed, died away, leaving behind it this peculiar stillness, with nothing good in it; it held only the memory of misfortune, and of more to come.

"And thank you for bringing me home," she persisted, undeterred. "I gave you a lot of trouble, driving me to the hospital and back. But I honestly don't think I could have driven, right then."

All this he ignored, impaling her with a level look and demanding, "You still don't know what's responsible for this condition of your mother's? You're going to stand there and tell me you don't know?"

Her look, exhausted and passive, only roused him, by some perversity, to goading her the more relentlessly. "Yes, and you've known all along," he accused. "If you'd told me before, all this might not have happened."

She shook her head faintly; it exasperated him past endurance.

"Don't shake your head," he said harshly.

"You stood by – just stood by and let it happen."

She raised her eyes and regarded him in silence; beautiful hazel eyes, he noticed, with the part of him that was not infuriated with her.

"It was bound to come," she said finally. "No one could stop it – not you or anyone else. You don't know what you're talking about, that's all."

He was taken back, but only for a moment.

"And why don't I?" he demanded. "Because you wouldn't tell me what you knew."

"I couldn't. I tell you I couldn't."

"What do you mean, you couldn't?" He had flung off his customary restraint of voice and manner. "Are you trying to make me believe there's something so frightful in your mother's life that it couldn't be talked about? That, my dear young lady, is an idiotic assumption – melodramatic nonsense." Her composure was breaking up, he saw with satisfaction; he wanted to break that stubborn calm, shatter it to pieces. "Your mother's led a conventional life, you've only to look at her to know it. To suggest that there's something about her that *really* can't be talked about, especially to a doctor –" he transfixed her with a hard, angry look. "Or maybe you thought so. But why not consult someone else? why consider your judgment final? Does it occur to you that in anything so serious, you had no right to be the sole judge?"

"I couldn't do anything," she managed to gasp, "but what I did do." She had the desperate look of being pushed into a corner; in her self-defense was an unspoken plea for mercy.

"All this is your fault," he threw at her brutally.

"No." Her voice wavered, broke. "No."

"You took it on yourself to make the decisions," he overbore her. "You're responsible for everything that's happened to your mother."

Her face broke up; she hid it quickly in her hands. Violent sobs, almost noiseless, began shaking her as she stood before him, her shoulders and head despairingly bowed. He had not counted on so complete a victory, nor on feeling such swift and troubling compunction.

"Ann." He put his hands on her bowed shoulders; she straightened with unexpected quickness and force, throwing off his touch, and uncovered her face, tearstained but inimical now, aloof. For a moment they regarded each other like enemies.

His next utterance was completely unexpected, not more to her than to himself.

"You saw me – out here – the other day," he blurted, not mentioning Connie; he knew it was unnecessary. As he sensed her inward retreat from him, he pursued, "You did, didn't you?"

"Yes," she said uncompromisingly.

"Listen." With the same unbelief he heard his voice in urgent self-justification before this immature girl, in all the priggishness of her youth and inexperience. "Listen. Did you ever do anything senseless – anything wrong or dishonest – even shameful? Did you?"

"Yes." She answered with the same forthrightness, with no tinge of equivocation or hesitancy.

"And then – after you'd done it – you couldn't imagine what had possessed you in the first place, you couldn't imagine why you'd done what you did? Did you ever feel like that? did that ever happen to you?"

"Yes." A marvelous, resuscitating warmth was restoring her to life. For the first time, experiencing the deliciousness of intimate conversation with a man, part of her nestled to this felicity, while another part of her – the wounded, humiliated part – retreated warily.

"Why are you telling me this?" she demanded.

This silenced him utterly for a moment. Why, indeed? Men talked in this fashion to women whose good opinion was important to them, women with whom they were in love, whom they were about to marry or wanted to marry. Not one of these considerations applied in his case; in the first place she was much too young for him, even if he were in love with her, which he was not — or was he? the sudden possibility, even remote, shook him to an astonishing degree.

He found his voice once more.

"Why am I telling you this?" he repeated. "Because — because I'm a little tired of being condemned every time you look at me. It gets tiresome," he repeated. "You still have a lot to learn."

She averted her eyes; a light went out in her face, leaving it quenched and bleak. Irritated at feeling himself, somehow, culpable, he said abruptly, "I'll have to be going now — I'll be in touch with you." He nodded at her where she stood unmoving, and turned toward the door.

"Doctor," she said behind him, as if unwilling. He stopped dead at once, with a half-formed expectation, an illogical hope. "Please give me something to make me sleep."

"Oh." He turned toward her again, feeling a momentary let-down, a cold disappointment.

"Well, I think I have something with me." As he opened his bag, she said, "I've been taking Calmolin, but it's all gone. But anything you can give me, even if it isn't very strong . . . Calmolin knocks me right out."

"These are stronger than Calmolin," he said, and tipped a solitary tablet onto the hall table. "If you're all that sedative-prone, better just take half of it."

"Thank you," she murmured, and neither moved nor spoke as he let himself out. Then at once she went up quickly to Myra's room, and began looking.

She found it sooner than she had expected — five compact oblong packages, buried in a drawerful of lace, silk and satin froth. She had no need to tear a corner of the paper to tell her what it was.

For a long few moments she stood looking at it, worried and frowning. Tomorrow morning, as early as possible, she would take it back to the bank and hand it to Mr. Hulse; but for the moment there was nothing to be done. All that money must stay in the house overnight. Before she shut the drawer she looked at it again, in a kind of wonderment. There it lay, the seed, flower and fruit of Connie's blackmail, of Myra's lost battle, of her — perhaps — final illness. . . .

261

She closed the drawer quickly, went downstairs, picked up the tablet and shut herself in her room. Again the peculiar silence of the house came home to her, the stricken silence following upon calamity and presaging yet more calamity. . . . Bessie was asleep upstairs, she knew, but all the same the house felt empty, empty, with an emptiness – instinct told her – final done-for. This habitation and all it contained, animate or inanimate, had changed; and this change was its ending.

She shivered, and decided to take the whole tablet.

CHAPTER 24

As he went home after office-hours, Ann
Walworth was present in his mind — what part
of it, at least, that he could spare from driving,
for it had begun to sleet, vicious javelins of
mixed sleet and snow, driving down hard at a
slight unvarying angle. Briskly the windshield
wipers clicked in their hemicyclic orbit; before
they could make the return trip, a woolly
dappling piled up on the glass. If it froze
before morning, he thought, there would be
hell to pay.

He reached his apartment and went straight
to bed in spite of its being comparatively early;
but he had had a long day, and was to assist at
an operation at seven-thirty tomorrow morning, so it was important to get a good night's
sleep. But sleep retreated from him. Ann was
in his mind again, with a persistence he was
unable to define as irritating or attractive. The
truth was, it had been one of those days — they
still returned occasionally — one of those days

haunted by a painfully vivid recollection of Linda; at such times his mood darkened restlessly, his hunted thoughts taking refuge where they could. This was his reason – of course – for thinking of Ann; she deserved better, poor young thing, than serving as an antidote to another girl.

Deliberately he set the two side by side, Ann beside Linda. Linda was a beauty, of course, Ann faded away beside her . . . but curiously, when he came to think of it, it was Linda who seemed to fade beside Ann, her discontented loveliness made insignificant by something about the other girl, some distinct and positive quality of warmth . . . but Linda, he thought, with a swiftly-recurring pain, Linda was so exquisitely made, a white-and-gold Mayflower, fragrant . . . yes, his commonsense added coldly, and spoiled and unpredictable and ruthlessly selfish, for at this distance of time he found he could be dispassionate. Ann continued to stand before him in a sort of growing luminousness, as the other girl paled. You could go to her and be helped in your need . . . plenty of people in trouble would recognize this quality of compassion in her, during her lifetime. Too bad she was so extremely young . . . then it dawned on him. She was certainly as old as Linda; why did he constantly think of her as barely grown-up? Of course — it was the extreme, almost naive candidness of her eyes, the freshness of her face, the unworldliness of her manner, without self-consciousness or desire to impress.

This novel awareness of her as a young woman, not a girl, unloosed in him a tide of feeling so urgent as to seem that it had only waited for this barrier — his erroneous idea of her age — to be withdrawn. A sudden tenderness took possession of him, and for an instant he had the elated feeling of a man who had found gold. Until — with dismay and disappointment — he felt the emotion cool and dwindle. Did he love her? it seemed not. Was he about to love her? He had no idea. There was too much confusion in him still, too much involvement with another image. Apparently he was one of those tiresome characters who took things hard, who was unable to throw off a relationship easily and take up with another as easily.

He turned over restlessly, and lay waiting for something, for some sudden enlightenment that would push him toward Ann or away from her, some moment of final clarification. He made himself void of thought, having no desire to think; he wanted to *feel*, to know himself, in some anaesthetized area, alive once more. But what dawned on him, for no reason, was an unexpected series of pictures, increasingly disturbing. He saw Ann and himself in the hall; around them was the stillness of the stricken house, in which nothing moved. He saw himself giving her the sedative, he saw her taking it, then lying heavily asleep, robbed by the drug of the sleeper's solitary defense, the ability to wake quickly. Helpless she lay there in the empty house . . . no, not empty, for he knew that Bessie lived in, but Bessie was two flights up in her own oblivion, the deep sleep of the hard worker. Then suddenly he could see, as circumstantial as if thrown by a film-projector, the front door of the Walworth house. The figure approaching it was less clear, but its stealthiness, even in the dark, was evident . . . he dismissed the image; it returned again and again, each time with a greater clarity. And always, within this clarity, moved the obscure figure, only half-emergent from its shadow, its malign aura . . . violently he flung back the bedclothes and got up, cursing to himself as he dressed. The thought of phoning her he dismissed; he wanted to *see* her, to see that she was all right, whether she thought him crazy or not, this long after midnight. As he got into his car he saw that the snow and sleet had stopped, but the streets looked very wet, and the cold was deepening rapidly and perceptibly. What the combination meant was only too evident.

As he drove the few miles as quickly as possible, he was still ridden, not by the image, but by the fear it had left behind it, a fear that kept increasing, however he scoffed at it . . . he became aware of a glare in the sky in the direction of Three Elms, which he was approaching. An absolute, leaden certainty smote him; as he tore into Old Mill Drive he was unsurprised by the crowd, the fire engines, the parked cars of onlookers, the acrid smell, unsurprised even by Myra's house. This was a curious spectacle, with its first floor more or less intact as far as he could see, and its second floor not burning any more, but still incandescent, with huge plumes of angry white steam hissing volcanically off its surface wherever the hoses struck. Nothing could be alive in that house, which had contained only two heavily-sleeping women.

His brusque doctor's voice and thrusting arm got him through the crowd in short order; the ground was soaking-wet and thick with a tangle of huge rubber serpents.

"There're in there," said the fire-chief, indicating a neighboring house fifty or sixty feet away. As Ralph began shoving toward it, a middle-aged man joined him.

"I'm a neighbor — name's Harmon," he said, keeping up with Ralph's rapid stride. "They're over at my house. You're — ?"

"Doctor," said Ralph.

"Well, that mightn't be a bad idea," said Mr. Harmon. He unlocked the front door, ushered Ralph into the hall, indicated a curtained doorway. "In there," he said. "Doctor." he explained to Mrs. Harmon, who had appeared from whatever point of vantage commanded the spectacle next door.

"Just call me if you want anything, doctor," said Mrs. Harmon, but he had already vanished between the drapes.

She lay on a sofa with a blanket thrown over her, but as Ralph stood beside her, her eyes opened. Their expression was slightly dazed; she focussed vaguely, with perceptible effort. After a moment, however, she found him; her gaze took hold of him intently, but he could see her half-aware look and the enormous dilation of the pupils.

"Were you hurt anywhere?" he said slowly and distinctly. "Burns? anything like that?" She seemed not to take it in; he repeated, "Are you hurt anywhere?"

"I hurt everywhere." Her voice was fast and

slurred as if talking in her sleep, her articulation trammeled by the drug — which, like alcohol, also melted from her tongue all hesitancies and inhibitions. "I hurt all over with loving you. I love you so, and it hurts all the time. Please," she besought him, "please come down nearer. You're so far away."

Was it the drug speaking, or she herself, he wondered, as he got down on his knees beside her.

"You were always so far away," her murmured plaint went on. "So far, far away."

"Are you all right?" he whispered. "Are you really all right?"

"I could be." In slow-motion, and unhandily, she extricated one hand from beneath the blanket and let it rest against his cheek. "Hold me," she entreated. "Hold me."

He hesitated, then put his arms around her gently and tentatively. This strange passage — with a girl half-under the combined effects of shock and sedation, perhaps hardly knowing what she was doing — had an unreal quality, dream-like. But through her nearness and warmth, a soreness in him was healing, dissolving, and that was no dream.

"I know exactly what I'm doing," she said suddenly, defiant and quite loud, as though reading his thoughts. Her hand continued to rest on his cheek. "Kiss me," she said. "Please kiss me."

He kissed her gently, then again, with restrained urgency, and murmured, "Go to sleep. You're half-asleep anyway."

"I'm not." She repudiated the idea absolutely, with heavy lids. "If I sleep, I'll . . . I'll lose you." But her voice fell away all at once, sleep came up and drowned her on the last word. He disengaged his arms cautiously, rose, and stood looking down at her, confusedly moved but disturbed by the thought of tomorrow, when she — more likely than he — might waken and repudiate all this. He stood a moment longer, then moved noiselessly out of the room and into the unfamiliar hall. Here a woman stood waiting for him.

"Hello, Bessie," he said. He had forgotten altogether this second occupant of the gutted house, who answered in her composed voice, "Evenin', doctor." She was a good-looking colored woman with a competent and rather hard manner; at the moment clad only in a coat thrown over a dressing-gown, and with a pocketbook hanging over one arm. Her coffee-and-cream face had gone yellow, with purple circles gouged out under her eyes, reflecting the shock and strain of the last hour.

"What happened?" he demanded, glad of

the chance to inform himself more fully. "Just how —?"

"I do' know how it started," rejoined Bessie. "I was sleeping pretty heavy I guess, and this sort of strangling feeling woke me up. Well, I grabbed my kimono and coat and purse and got out of there, the staircase wasn't burning yet but the banisters was hot and the steps was hot, I could feel them through my slippers. It was worst on the second floor, I could see that much, but I wasn't foolin' around to take notice particular, I'm telling *you*. Well, so I got downstairs, and Miss Ann's door was closed — but not locked, thank goodness — so I went in there and couldn't wake her up, she was right out as if she was drugged-like. So I pulled her out of bed an' into the hall, and by then she sort of come to — I mean she got on her feet but didn't know what was going on — so I just grabbed her bag an' coat an' got her out of the house. She came along all right, I just led her, like she was sleep-walkin'. So we came over here and Mr. Harmon he turned in the alarm."

"And you've no idea how it started," he pursued. Did she hesitate before answering, or not? A host of half-formed suspicions began jostling in his mind — only partly dissipated as she shook her head.

"No sir, 'specially on the second floor I

wouldn't know why. On the first floor there was Miss Ann, and on the third floor there was me — to account for somethin' happening — but on the second floor there was nobody since Mrs. Walworth she got took to the hospital, not a soul."

"I see." He cogitated, frowning and dissatisfied; his meditations were interrupted by Bessie.

"Doctor."

"Yes?"

"Miss Ann said a funny thing — to this fella that got in here, this reporter."

"What funny thing?"

"She didn't know who she was talkin' to," pursued Bessie. "I guess she thought she was talkin' to me. But she said she must go back in the house —" her voice became slow and puzzled "— and get her mother's money, or all the money would burn up —"

"Money!"

"That's what she said." Bessie entrenched herself visibly in her statement. "She was dazed pretty bad, but she said it — all the money would get burnt-up."

"Do you know what she was talking about?"

"Not me," she assured him, "but she said it to this reporter fella. *I* couldn't stop her talkin'. So I thought somebody ought to know."

"Well —" he frowned, cogitated again "— I gave her a sleeping-tablet before, and what with shock and so forth — she was probably wandering a little. That was a wonderful job you did, Bessie," he added fervently. "Getting her out of the house. I'm glad you smelled the fire."

"So'm I," said Bessie dryly. "Wasn't ever anything much wrong with my smeller."

"Look, I know you're probably dead on your feet," he appealed. "But sleep near her tonight, could you?"

"I'll ask Mrs. Harmon can I sit in one of them big chairs in the living-room." The peculiar readiness in her voice rather surprised him. "I can sleep sittin' up."

"Thanks." With a half-misgiving he pressed a bill into her hand, and was relieved when she did not seem offended. "I'll be here early tomorrow, and we'll arrange things. Goodnight, Bessie."

"Goodnight, doctor." Had she hesitated again before answering? He looked at her with inquiry; she said nothing further, so he turned toward the door — and heard her voice behind him.

"Doctor."

He glanced over his shoulder. Then, as her aspect was borne in on him, he turned full around – knowing, by some instinct, that she was about to say something for which he had been subconsciously waiting. "Yes, Bessie?"

"There was a kind of funny thing happened –" she sounded tentative, however, "– happened in our house a couple weeks back. I do' know, maybe it didn't mean nothing, but maybe –"

"What funny thing?" he interrupted. "What happened?"

"Mrs. Connie – Mrs. Connie Walworth – she come in the house one day." She spoke as if half-unwilling, watching him out of shrewd dark eyes, ready to back-pedal at the first shade of unfriendliness or discouragement. "She come in the front door with her own key – that's something I didn't know she had – an' she went in Miss Ann's room an' closed the door."

She stopped; he waited an instant, then said, "Yes?"

"Well, that's all, kind of," admitted Bessie, a little apologetically. "She was in there a couple minutes, not more'n five minutes anyway, an' then she went out. So what I was wonderin', could it maybe have anything to do with – with –"

"With the fire? How long ago was it that you saw her?"

"Two weeks ago, anyway." Her uncertain air increased. "Two weeks, maybe pretty near three."

"I don't see," he reflected slowly, out loud, "I don't see how anything she did that long ago could have any bearing on this. Did you hear anything when she was in Miss Ann's room?"

"Not a thing – an' I went out in the hall an' listened, too. I did sort of hear a sound like she was pokin' up the fire in the fireplace, but that was all. An' I went in there after she lef' an had me a good look around, believe you me, but I didn't see nothin'. But all the same I was wondering –"

"Did you mention this to Mrs. Walworth – I mean your Mrs. Walworth? or to Miss Ann?"

"No, *sir*," she answered flatly. "Mrs. Connie is Mrs. Walworth's daughter-in-law, an' maybe Mrs. Walworth gave her the key. It's their business. You got to be careful what you say when you can't prove nothing," she assured him, out of a profoundly-ingrained caution, " 'specially about white people."

"Mh'm." He reflected a moment before putting – belatedly – the key question that occurred to him. "Bessie – just why do you think Mrs. Connie had anything to do with the fire?"

"If you'd seen the way she sneaked in the

house, doctor," she answered. "Soft an' quiet-like, not makin' a sound. I wouldn't of known anything about it, except I was in the pantry right then an' the door was open, just a fraction, an' I saw her, all right — pussyfootin', lookin' all around to see if anybody was there. Nobody," she declared, "nobody that come sneakin' in that quiet ever meant any good."

Something about her expression prompted him to ask, "You don't like Mrs. Connie, do you, Bessie?"

She retreated at once into her usual noncommittal reserve and answered laconically, "I guess she's all right." But in the instant before she answered he had seen, in those cold eyes, a passing gleam — of simple, uncomplicated hatred, or he missed his guess.

"Why don't you like her?" he pursued.

"I ain't said I don't like her," she answered coolly, at which he smiled, but could not tell whether there was the faintest answering smile in those well-controlled features.

"Well, Bessie —" he reflected again before continuing, "I've heard of delayed-action gadgets that would set a fire — everyone has, of course — but only of the kind that would work after a number of hours, not after a number of days or weeks." He recollected something else, suddenly. "In any case, you said she went in

276

Miss Ann's room?"

"Yessir."

"But the fire was upstairs," he reminded her. She was silent a moment, then assented with a disappointed air, "Yes, that's so."

"We'd better leave it at that, for the present," he said. "They'll go in there tomorrow, after it's cooled down enough, and maybe they'll find out what started it. Well, goodnight, Bessie — I'll be around early tomorrow."

He let himself out of the house, whose owners were not in evidence, and went down a slippery walk to his car, pondering Bessie's story. Glad as he would have been to find a tangible resting-place for his suspicions, he could not for the life of him think of any delayed-action incendiary device that would act after a two- or three-week period. . . .

Five minutes later, with a sense of anticlimax, he was knocking again at Harmons' door. Almost at once Bessie opened it.

"My car won't start." He spoke softly, afraid of disturbing Ann in the next room. "Could you ask Mr. or Mrs. Harmon if I can phone a garage from here?"

"I go ask'r —" Bessie began, and was interrupted by a voice from the living-room.

"Ralph!" Ann called. Her voice was urgent, and a little clearer. "Ralph!"

He went through the drapes and beheld a girl with flushed cheeks and a surprisingly wide-awake look — though he knew this wakefulness was spasmodic, likely to be swallowed up by sleep at any moment.

"Did you say your car won't start?" she demanded. "Take mine — take my car. Look in my bag — Bessie saved it. There're garage keys and car keys — on the same ring. The garage isn't burned, is it? Take the keys," she insisted. "Bessie can go out with you and tell them it's all right, that I said you could have it."

He looked down into the unfamiliar complication of a woman's handbag, found and withdrew a keyring.

"Don't worry about your car," he said. "I'll take good care of it." In his mind he doubted utterly that she remembered anything of what had passed between them so short time before. His doubt was speedily dissipated.

"Come here," she begged breathlessly. "Please come here."

"Don't sit up." He put his arms around her; she flung hers around his neck. It was remarkable how much steam she could get up, even under the retarding and semi-cloudiness of the drug. They began kissing again, kisses short and hard and unsparingly ardent. And through all the strangeness of the attendant circumstances, the lateness of the hour, the strange house, the atmosphere of recent shock and confusion, they were overwhelmed, possessed, by something fearsomely lovely, too lovely to survive tomorrow. But they knew also, by some irrefutable illogic, that it would survive not only tomorrow but any number of tomorrows, a far-flung vista of them, dwindling into distance.

Against the force of his conviction the image of Linda broke and was whirled out of his mind finally and once for all, a straw doll scattered by the wind.

Cautiously he guided Ann's car down the driveway, noting that the crowd of sightseers had thinned out considerably. And no wonder, for if the snow and sleet had stopped altogether, the mercury had taken that precipitous downward plunge that he had foreseen; the cold, atrocious, struck through his clothes like so much wrapping-paper and laid an iron hand about his ribs. The street, wherever a light fell on it, gleamed black and satiny beneath a powdering of light snow or rime, its aspect incredibly treacherous. He debated putting on the chains, and decided not, in view of the short distance he had to drive.

Once in the street, it was as bad as he had

known it would be, and worse; the car moved with a horrible floating motion, with absolutely no sensation of ground beneath the wheels. The short run home was going to be a nightmare. Moving along in nerve-racking fashion, slipping and sliding, he nursed the wheel for a mile or so, hardly daring to touch the brake, until the lights of an all-night garage decided him. He would turn in there and have the chains put on.

Slowly and easily, in the deserted street, he turned left, blew his horn; in a moment the overhead door began rising. He started mounting the ramp of the garage – and felt nightmare, tangible, materialize between his two hands. The wheel went utterly loose; it felt incredibly awful, that sudden, complete cessation of pull or tension. Instinctively he switched off the engine and waited, helpless, as the car zigzagged backward off the ramp, went into a slow spin that carried it into the middle of the glassy street, veered to one side and back again . . . then came to rest, quietly, against the curb. That was all – except for the feeling in the pit of his stomach. Of all that might have happened, nothing, miraculously, had happened; the car had stopped without killing anyone or damaging anything.

Within the lighted garage, a couple of men

were running toward him.

It was curious to reflect that all that had been no further away than yesterday; yet his life had changed completely. The person who had changed it was installed, with Bessie, in a country inn nearby, a comfortable old place; and now it was after office-hours, past five and already quite dark, but in his mind was a warm illumination toward which he moved; he would be seeing her in a few minutes.

But as he let himself out the front door, there confronted him a big rangy man, hard-faced, in uniform.

"Dr. Markham?" said this man. "Dr. Ralph Markham? Sergeant Reading here, State Troopers. Talk to you a couple of minutes?"

Between annoyance and curiosity he was obliged to readmit them, switch on lights in his darkened waiting-room and office.

"Sit down," he said, and both of them sat. While the Sergeant regarded him noncommittally before beginning, Ralph had time to speculate on the occasion of this visit, and was left at a loss; he had been in no brush with the law that he knew of. The Sergeant answered his unspoken query.

"It's this car you left at the Arco garage yesterday," he said. "It ain't registered as belonging to you, Doc."

"It was lent me by the owner, Miss Ann Walworth," Ralph began, and was halted by the Sergeant's placidly-lifted hand.

"I know who it belongs to," he said.

"Well, what about it?" demanded Ralph, beginning to feel slightly impatient. "I told them to fix it and bill me — since I was driving when it went out of control. Where do you people come in on it?"

"We were called in on it," the Sergeant said amicably, "When the garage mechanics had a look at it, they called us right away. Car's been at the barracks garage all day, over to Pendleton. And believe me, it's had a going-over."

"But what for?" Ralph, as he spoke, felt a slight premonitory chill, he could not have said why. "What was wrong?"

"The wheel went dead on you, that right?" the Sergeant queried, and at Ralph's nod, "And it went dead because it'd been tampered with."

"What!?" But his stupefaction was succeeded swiftly by a cold, settled conviction.

"Sure thing." The Sergeant nodded with a sort of ominous pleasantry. "Monkey-business with the tie-rod ends. They didn't wear out, either — we found the marks of tools. Oh, it was done real smart — they were just touched-up, just partially weakened, sort of. After that, it's just a question of time until the thing gives way."

He ceased for a moment, observing benignantly the effect of this on Ralph.

"And what happens when it gives way," he resumed, "is anybody's guess. Maybe just you get it, or maybe it's a massacre — a dozen people, a busload, a trainload. And very likely the joker that dreamed this up —" he paused, with a momentary swelling of his jaw-muscles. "— this joker gets away with it, because if you smash up there's at least even chances you're on fire right away, and not enough left to prove anything." He paused; they were silent a moment.

"I'll be talking to Miss Walworth later," the Sergeant went on imperturbably, "but I figured with the fire they had there last night and everything, she wouldn't be in such good shape maybe. So I figured I'd make use of the time — talk to you first." He paused again, as if hopefully; Ralph said nothing.

"Who'd do a thing like that to Miss Walworth, doc?" he enquired softly. "Would you have any ideas?"

Ralph continued silent — well aware, however, that the other had instantly defined his silence as pregnant, not merely puzzled or empty. Nevertheless, still incredulous at what he had heard, he sat trying to pick his way through a crowding mass of considerations. Those bruises on Ann's face — made with something dangerously heavy, and eloquent of an encounter not far from murderous, eloquent also of a lethal enmity, a secret struggle — in whose atmosphere Myra was visibly wasting away and dying before his eyes. The nature of his conflict was still hidden from him, but he had not the slightest doubt as to the source and mainspring of the whole murky affair. Withdrawn into its shadows, yet faintly visible, was the well-known figure, like a slim elegant shark in its shadowy passage through deep water. . . .

And yet, his lack of positive information, coupled with the universal stubborn repugnance at turning informer, however justifiably. . . .

"How 'bout it, doc?" the Sergeant pressed cautiously. "You can save us a lot of time, maybe. Care to give us a line?"

"No," said Ralph decisively. "I don't know anything for sure. On the basis of supposition — or suspicion — I wouldn't care to give names."

The Sergeant sat up straight all at once, with a ludicrously disappointed air.

"Your giving a name," he expostulated, "won't hurt anyone that's innocent. Hell, doc, you needn't worry about that, if they're clean,

284

they're clean —"

"I'm sorry," Ralph interrupted. "If I knew anything for sure I'd be glad to help. But this way, no. I can't —" he broke off as the phone rang. "Excuse me a moment."

"Doctor? this Bessie." Hastily she reassured him. "Miss Ann's all right, I'm calling 'bout something else. That fire-chief, he just called up here, an' Miss Ann she asleep so I talked to him. They been in there, doctor — where the fire was."

"Did they find out what started it?"

"Yessir, doctor — they say it's the fireplace in Miss Ann's room."

"But the fire was upstairs."

"Ye', but they say it start from there all the same, they say the fire just happen to go up'ards instead of sideways. The chief he say the fireback it full of cracks, an' some of the cracks was so big he'd almost think they was opened up with something on purpose. He don't say they was, he just say they're awful big cracks."

She was silent a moment, so was he; unuttered between them lay the substance of last night's conversation.

"He say," Bessie resumed, "he say it just a question of time before enough heat get through and reach the wood an' all. Say, doctor, ain't it lucky Mrs. Walworth went to the hospital just a few hours before? The way it was when I saw it, she get roasted alive in there, yes, *sir.* Doctor," she added, "how Mrs. Walworth?"

"About the same, Bessie," he said. "I'll tell you when I see you — I'll be over in a few minutes."

"I'll tell Miss Ann." He thought he heard the ghost of a chuckle before she hung up.

He hung up also, and turned — with something in his aspect so purposeful that the Sergeant visibly plucked up heart again, and regarded him with hungry fixity. What had decided him was one sentence of Bessie's, striking on his ear in exact echo, almost, of something he had just heard.

He say it just a question of time until enough heat get through and reach the wood . . . and the Sergeant's *They were just partially weakened. After that, it's just a question of time until the thing gives way.*

Not that it constituted in itself any kind of proof, but as mere coincidence it was a little hard to swallow. Certainty smote him, illogical but absolute. The same method each time, he thought; the very same method. No direct attack, inviting direct suspicion; only a sly undermining, ratlike, with results so delayed as

286

to confuse the judgment and shield the perpetrator. And she had counted – both times – on the evidence being destroyed by fire; perhaps, as regarded the house, it was destroyed.

But the car's not burned up, lady, he thought. *We still have the car.*

"I've changed my mind," he informed the Sergeant, who was still waiting on his slightest word. "I'm going to give you a name. And while you're about it, take an expert over to Mrs. Walworth's on Old Mill Drive, where they had the fire last night, and have a look at the first-floor fireplace."

"We'll do that," the Sergeant assured him. He took out a notebook, held his pencil ready. "All right, doc – what was the name, now?"

CHAPTER 25

Connie sat at her breakfast-table, over her third cup of coffee, at four in the afternoon. Gil Hubbard had stayed the night, only leaving late that morning, so from ten o'clock on Connie had been catching up on sleep.

At the moment she sat in a delicious torpor of content and repletion; every now and then she yawned luxuriously. Then gradually, to her pleasant blankness of mind, there succeeded a slightly more active mental state, in which she began reviewing the highly satis-factory state of her life — all brought about by her own cleverness. Everything had turned out perfectly; everything was under control.

First, Myra — who had not yet come across with the money, it was true, but Connie had given her six weeks, of which only a month had gone by. Nevertheless, she would phone tomor-row and jog her memory — just a friendly reminder. She would pay up, of course, she had no choice. That disposed of Myra.

Secondly, Ann. In the warm, frowsty room, smelling of stale ash-trays, Connie chuckled aloud, suddenly. Any day now, she thought; any day. The little sneak must surely be hurt or mutilated somehow; Connie even felt that she would settle for a badly-burned or cut-up face. Yes, Ann was taken care of; it was just a question of which would work first, the doctored fireplace or the doctored car.

And last — her eyes hooded wickedly and the slightest smile curved her small mouth — last of all was the question of Ralph. There was no hurry about Ralph; her thoughts began playing about him lazily, speculatively, like prowling black panthers. She would attend to him, in her own good time. For instance, go to his office on pretext of consulting him, then tear her clothes suddenly and scream . . . a doctor never lived down a thing like that; guilty or exonerated, the question-mark would hang over him forever, the lingering doubts, the whispers . . . yes, she would see to him, but later.

Again her thoughts reverted to self-congratulation, as she compared her dire situation of a few months ago with the creamy present. Plenty of money in prospect, new clothes, a long trip somewhere; opportunities of frequenting places where one met men with money. And all this because of Archie's diary — because of his dream that she had been clever enough to raise up entire, out of mere fragments and hints. The smartest thing she had ever done in her life, catching onto that; she owed a lot to old Archie . . . and his dream. . . .

She sat up all at once, startled by a sudden flash of realization — which vanished before she could seize or define it. What had struck her so suddenly? What word had touched off what thought, that had flared up and gone out in darkness, all in an instant? Puzzled, she began groping backward in her mind. What had she been thinking of, just the moment before? The dream . . . Archie's dream; that was it. And again the word *dream* seemed to flash over her mental landscape a sort of lightning, revealing a too-short glimpse of curious shapes, indefinable, on its horizon. . . .

"My God," she thought astounded, almost awed. "My God." Separate facts fell together, lined up in a strange sequence to form a stranger whole . . . it had never before struck her, and still was not quite clear in her mind. Frowning, she set herself to trace the shadowy outline.

Archie had suffered from a recurrent nightmare. Immediately upon his death, Luanna had started to dream — yes, on the very night of his death; Connie had seen her the next day after, and Mrs. Donlan had commented on the violence of this disturbance, and on the rarity of her dreaming at all. Senile Luanna, dreaming that she had stolen . . .

Then, shortly after, Theo's complaint of a dream that had harried him for the last few weeks — when Archie had been dead just about that long; Theo's dream, apparently, following directly upon the death, like Luanna's. *The same dream all the time,* she heard his half-whining voice. Luanna and Theo, accomplices in a long-past murder, beginning to dream just after Archie had died . . . coincidence? maybe, but pretty funny coincidence, all the same. Connie experienced a slight chill. What she was thinking, but lacked the power to put in words, was . . . well, it sounded crazy, but it had happened. It was as though Luanna and Theo had *inherited* Archie's dream as soon as he was dead; as if he had bequeathed it to them or wished it on them, like a curse or something. Or as though the dream, over all these years, had taken on a separate life of its own; as though, deprived by death of the body it had tenanted, it had gone knocking at other skulls for admittance. . . .

But — her memory suddenly objected —

Luanna and Theo had not inherited the *same* dream; theirs were different from Archie's. This seemed for a moment to put a crimp in her theory of the bequeathed dream . . . and then it struck her; struck with a new impact, raising gooseflesh all over her. Wait though, wait, she thought, and began reviewing the three different dreams.

Archie, eternally on guard before the closed door.

Luanna, stealing the hypodermic.

Theo, forever riding with Mrs. Schermerhorn.

She nodded to herself, slowly, affirmatively, with a slight shiver. Yes, it all added up. *Each of the three Gedneys, in the life of the dream, forever performing his part in the crime;* forever repeating the same actions over and over; forever harnessed to the treadmill of the deed. . . . And these dreams had been her only clues; they were the shadowy guideposts that had beckoned her along the almost-obliterated trail of a long-buried, unsuspected murder. . . .

Connie felt another and a colder chill. You could practically call it supernatural; what else? for this literal world was enmeshed in a tenuous, invisible, yet ever-present web of inexplicable happenings such as omens, clairvoyance, precognition, telepathy; no one could explain these things, but no one could deny them either.

Then an inconsistency occurred to her. *Why had Myra not dreamed?* or at least Connie had never heard of her doing so. For to complete and round out her theory, Myra should have the worst dream of all, since she had done the actual murder . . . but how, *how?* Again that question, maddening, assailed Connie with all its power of mystification. How had Myra done it?

She pondered for the next few minutes to no effect, then dismissed the subject impatiently. She had thought about it too much in the last months; the hell with it. Languidly she rose, lit a cigarette, then decided to step out and investigate the contents of the mailbox beside the gatepost. The flag was up, she could see from the window.

The box contained only a newspaper – the small local daily, to which Lydia subscribed. Not worth the exertion of walking up to the big house; she took it back to her own place, threw it on the table. It was while she was clearing away her breakfast dishes and an accumulation of ashtrays that the headline caught her eye.

FIRE GUTS HOME;
ILLNESS SAVES OWNER

Jan. 27. Fire broke out around midnight yesterday at the home of Mrs. Myra Walworth, Old Mill Drive, Three Elms Twp., almost totally destroying the second and third floors. Only a few hours previously Mrs. Walworth had been removed to Baylor Memorial Hospital, after a heart-attack. Occupants of the house were Miss Ann Walworth, daughter, and Bessie Seney, maid. Both escaped unhurt. The alarm was turned in at 12.27 A.M. by George Harmon, a neighbor. The Eagle Fire Company responded and brought the blaze under control after prolonged effort, during which Wendville Hook and Ladder also responded to the alarm. Destruction of effects on the second and third floors was total, with considerable damage to first-floor furnishings from water and smoke. Total damage is estimated between $25,000 and $30,000. Fire-chief Faust ascribed the outbreak to a faulty fireplace on the first floor.

It is reported but not confirmed that a large sum of money, kept in Mrs. Walworth's room on the second floor, was also included in the loss. Mrs. Walworth's condition is reported as serious at Baylor Memorial.

Connie slowly lowered the paper; then, her arms and legs going nerveless all at once, she sat down suddenly. After a few moments she raised the paper, read the item again. There was no need, however; the significant part of it had eaten into her brain like acid. The money in Myra's room . . . it was the blackmail money, of course, being accumulated for her. All that fun, ease, luxury, *security* — all gone up in smoke, reduced to a mass of char and ash. . . .

The room darkened more and more; she made no move to light a lamp, but sat on motionless in the deepening obscurity, her face suddenly contracted and pinched, with hollow cheeks, half-open mouth, unseeing eyes . . . in the total collapse of her despair she had not even the heart to speculate on the accident of under-floor or between-wall drafts by which the fire had attacked, not the first floor, but the second. And Myra inaccessible now, in the hospital; and if she died, inaccessible forever, and the diary reduced to mere waste paper, fuel for the trash-burner. . . .

Slowly there penetrated her stupor realization that someone was knocking at the door, only a few feet away from her. By day they could have seen her through the glass panel; but now, knowing herself invisible in the darkness, she made no move to rise. Let them knock; they would stop after awhile and go away.

But the knocking did not stop; it went on and on, loud and full of certainty, proclaiming someone's knowledge that she was there. Now its quality altered a little; to its determined and regular note was added an accent of . . . yes, of authority. A faint rage began stirring in her, far down, beneath the ruin and debris of her shipwreck. Who dared raise that ungodly racket? She would tell them a thing or two, whoever it was; it would feel good to rip up someone, leave them in shreds. The nerve of them, the God-damned nerve. . . .

She yanked at the chain of a lamp, then darted to the door in a fury.

CHAPTER 26

Myra lay in bed, for the moment free from pain. Only she wondered feebly at her degree of weakness, for this, like no ordinary weakness, gripped you in every limb, nailed you to your bed, made all effort, even the raising of one's eyelids, mountainous. But otherwise the nurse had made her comfortable, and for all her feebleness, her brain raced and churned, uncontrollably active.

Her thoughts were exhaustingly repetitive, circling around and around the misfortunes of the last few months. With this went an endless incredulity and outrage at the blow that fortune had dealt her, in exhuming and confronting her with that long-buried episode. To think, only to think, of its blowing up in her face twelve years later! and all through the sheer, crazy accident of Connie's getting her claws on Archie's diary. If that wasn't rotten luck, thought Myra, with grief, amazement and injury; she would like to know what it was.

The spitefulness of fate, the malice of events! For the disaster that had overtaken her was due in no sense to any fault of hers, or to any flaw in her original plan, but entirely to the random circumstance of Archie's nitwit habit of scribbling in little green books. How could she have guarded against such a contingency? Impossible; no one could foresee everything. For her plan *had* been perfect, it had been perfectly carried through, it had succeeded a hundred percent. Even now, reviewing its successive steps, she could not withhold the proud, fond smile of the creator.

When Margaret Gedney — who was after all only their stepmother — refused to die; when she promised, with crass inconsiderateness, to live on and on, past a reasonable age; then it became imperative, justifiable, to do something about it.

My wife the aforesaid Margaret Gedney shall have the use and enjoyment of the income from my aforesaid estate during her lifetime. At her decease, my aforesaid estate shall be divided equally, per stirpes, among my four children, Luanna, Archibald, Theodore and Myra . . . and at eighty-four the aforesaid Margaret was still using and enjoying the aforesaid income, and gave every indication of using and enjoying it for years to come. At this rate, they would inherit only when they themselves were dodderers, long past the capacity to have fun with money; they could buy themselves expensive funerals, and that would be about it. And their lives, at this period, were so intolerably drab and limited! Herself, trying to put up a front (and doing it very well, too) on Tony's mediocre income and the remains of her first husband's estate; Archie, bored sick with his instructorship at a third-rate college; Luanna, withering on the vine at home; Theo, a not-very-successful bond salesman. All these people, panting on the threshold of a larger existence, yet restrained from stepping over — kept out of their own money — by the existence of one useless, unwanted old woman!

It was she alone, out of all of them, who had had the guts to do something about it. She had called a conference . . . even now she had to smile faintly, thinking of that first council of war. The horrified protests, when they understood what she was driving at; the incredulous exclamations, the sanctimonious refusals! Through this moral façade she had broken at once, without the least trouble. They all *wanted* it to happen, the hypocrites — but without themselves being involved; they wanted to wake up some morning and find that it had been brought about, obligingly, with no need to dirty their own hands nor be embarrassed by inconvenient knowledge. This wishful thinking she had also demolished, pointing out with utmost explicitness that if they were to benefit in common, they must take the risks in common; it was a joint enterprise, or nothing. She had urged, cajoled, she had pushed and fought those flabby wills into line, and one by one they had weakened, as she had instinctively known from the first they would. Oh yes, she knew them.

And then — having wrung from them their weak-kneed promises of co-operation — she found herself immobilized on the very threshold of action, brought to a dead standstill. Not that her purpose flagged, not for the fraction of an instant. But having reviewed the usual means of murder — poison, shooting, stabbing, suffocation — she found none that met her purpose in the slightest degree. She had no wish to court the electric chair; she wanted to live and spend her quarter-of-a-million dollars. No, what she wanted was something that would give the appearance of natural death and leave no traces — and what this might be, she could not even remotely imagine. Also, how to surmount the obstacle of the old woman's nurse, that ever-present busybody and chatterbox. . . . She felt completely at a standstill, and was beginning to despair.

Then she met Raúl.

Raúl O'Connor; even now a fugitive glow warmed her at the thought of him. Tall, superbly built, full of hell, very dark but with startling blue eyes, he had been born in the Argentine of an Irish father and a South American mother. An O'Connor who spoke English with a Spanish accent; this always seemed to her screamingly funny, and, somehow, exciting. He was younger than she – at the time she had been over fifty – but almost as pretty as she had ever been, appearing about forty. Raúl, explaining that red-haired women were his fatality, had gone completely off his head about her. The ghost of a reminiscent smile passed over her face. A nerve-shaking experience, to find yourself in bed with him – for beneath his cosmopolitan gloss, Raúl was a complete savage, making Tony Walworth and every other man she had had look like so many limp rags. And his talk was as good as a circus, he had lived in so many places and done so many amazing things. For instance, he had represented his country in Fascist Italy, then later in Nazi Germany; he had known Mussolini and Hitler personally and had attended many of Goering's wild parties, where the unchained pet leopard created a slight jumpiness among the naked women. With his German hosts – who sounded like *divine* people – he had been thoroughly at home and had the time of his life; they had toured him around everywhere and had showed him every-thing – down to Goebbels' secret museum whose very existence was known to hardly any people, even the best-informed; few Germans, and only the most-exceptionally favored foreign visitors, were admitted. The museum was the best of Raúl's stories; as good as a horror movie, deliciously scary. Here Goebbels – who was very scientific-minded, in fact a great scientist in his own way, Raúl assured her – housed a collection of curiosities demon-strating various unique experiments, by German doctors, on chosen subjects from concentration-camps. There was a series of human heads showing that, by application of sub-zero colds, you could shrink the brain to the size of an egg; the tops of all the heads lifted off conveniently, so that you could peer in and see it. As a final and really terrific macabre touch, the mouths of all the heads were sewn together. The museum also con-tained the results – in the form of one or two whole cadavers, photographs, and records – of other curious and original experiments, such as hypodermic injection, directly into the bloodstream, of various kinds of gases, even ordinary cooking-gas – which, Raúl had been authoritatively informed, killed without leaving discoverable traces in autopsy. Yes, it was as good as a show, listening to Raúl, darling Raúl. He would have married her if she had had a million; she could see his point of view and find it entirely reasonable. They had parted the best of friends, and he had married an Argentine coffee-heiress in three months.

It was shortly after Raúl's departure for greener fields that she had dropped in at the Gedney house on one of her regular visits – ostensibly to see the old lady, but in reality to keep tabs on her condition. Upon that day Mrs. Donlan, admitting her, had announced that the doctor had just finished with Mrs. Gedney.

"I'll go right up," said Myra.

Mrs. Donlan disappeared, but Myra did not go up; she was staring into a doctor's bag, which, standing half-open on the console, revealed something that gripped her attention. She would have called it a monster hypodermic; she was not to know that she was looking at an intravenous syringe, with its enormous glass reservoir and big needle. On the instant of seeing it, a certain detail of Raúl's narrative, half-forgotten, suddenly leaped into her mind, clear, tremendous and significant. That great big hypodermic . . . and cooking-gas, always available; one commodity there was no need to hunt in drugstores. . . . And there, all at once, and complete in every detail, was her plan.

The sound of running water ceased in the nearby lavatory, and she was up the stairs and out of sight on the landing before the doctor emerged. She had made no attempt to secure the hypodermic; she would not have touched it with a ten-foot pole. No least suspicious circumstance must accompany *any* of her visits here. Also, her plan, already functioning, had neatly quartered the responsibility among the four of them, like the apple in the schoolbook. Luanna lived in the house, therefore had most opportunity of knowing the doctor's comings and goings; Luanna would secure the hypodermic, thus implicating herself to the necessary degree. The others would receive their instructions in due course.

Luanna's reception of her assignment had been, for so weak a reed, surprisingly turbulent; she had all but refused, weeping desperately: But some days later, dithering in protest, she had brought Myra the big hypodermic.

Now began, on Myra's part, a series of

bizarre and furtive experiments, carried out in her kitchen on the maid's day off – unseen as far as she knew, but Luanna must have caught sight of them, at one time or another; Connie had terrorized her with this fact most of all. She had acquired a familiarity with her proposed weapon, practising the manipulation of the plunger, separating the needle from the glass reservoir. In this it was easy to create a vacuum by sucking it until her lips clung; then she hastily sealed it with her finger, inverted it over a turned-on-gas-jet for some moments, then quickly stoppered it with the needle. The inside of the glass chamber failed to reveal, by any clouding or fogging, whether it were filling, yet it stank to Heaven when she smelled it; she had to conclude that the vacuum did fill with gas. The question was, did it hold enough to do the damage? The syringe was the biggest she had ever seen; the topmost figure on its calibrated scale read 150. After repeated trials she became restive, anxious to put to the test her weapon with its home-made lethal charge. If it failed to work – then she would simply have to put a pillow over the old lady's face, that was all, and hope for the best. That nurse, though, always underfoot . . . she had pondered a moment, then picked up the phone and called Theo.

The next day they had descended upon their old home in force; she, Archie, and Theo. Luanna, by arrangement with Theo, would be removed from the house at the crucial period . . . at this moment Myra felt herself drowning, sinking away into blackness. Dimly she wanted to call the nurse, who was there at her bedside, she knew — but the effort was mountainous and crushing, impossible. . . .

Now she felt herself strangely suspended in a twofold state: she was asleep and awake, at the same time. That is, she knew she was asleep, but on the other hand she had the most vivid sense of being on her feet, strong and well and lively, walking rapidly. . . .

She was walking down the second-floor corridor of the Gedney house, with Archie. Leaving him on guard at their stepmother's door, she went into the room. Margaret Gedney's resolute old face was calm with sleep; this was luck, but how long would it last? If only she would stay asleep until it was all over, what a quantity of trouble it would save. . . .

Myra took the syringe from her handbag, and readied it. She would thrust it, she had decided, into the mark of a previous injection — Mrs. Gedney, she knew, received daily shots. But she could see no such mark. The old lady's arm, in half-sleeves, lay outside the light coverlet, but turned palms down, concealing the underarm. This was the worst break that could possibly be, for now she must touch the sleeper, previous to making the actual attempt; there was no help for it.

Softly, softly, her eyes riveted on her step-mother, she took one limp hand, gently turned it . . . on the aged brownish underarm, heavily mottled black-and-blue, there was only one prick that looked fresh. It was as much as she had hoped for. With one hand she laid a light, steadying touch on the arm, with the other advanced the needle's point to the mark of the previous injection. . . .

Margaret Gedney woke up.

Not incompletely, not confusedly; her eyes opened wide, with full awareness and compre-hension. Myra, panicky, tightened her grip on the thin old arm, clumsily rammed home the big needle, violently pushed down the plunger . . . and that was all. Except for that one bad moment when the old devil had had to wake up — she would, Myra thought bitterly — the plan had worked, the wonderful idea for which she could thank Raúl. In her ignorance she could hardly know that the needle had failed to reach a vein, that the gas had dissipated harm-lessly from the tissues; that the old lady, waking to the light-blue eyes of murder looking down at her, had simply died of shock and fright. . . .

Now in her dream Myra was experiencing another consciousness of duality. She was still Myra, but in some peculiar way she was Margaret Gedney too, in the moment of her death; she could feel a havoc in her veins, a rending pain in her chest and arms, then a tremendous blackness, cataclysmic, engulfing her . . . and now Raúl was there again, and he was tickling her, tickling her all over, and it was excruciating, you could die of it, die laughing, he was tickling her to death and she couldn't make him stop. . . .

She smiled.